GARDEN OF THE GODS

Other Books by Stephen J. Stirling

Shedding Light on the Dark Side

Persona Non Grata

GARDEN OF THE GODS

STEPHEN J. STIRLING

SWEETWATER
BOOKS

An imprint of Cedar Fort, Inc.
Springville, Utah

ISBN 13: 978-1-4621-1938-7

Published by Sweetwater Books, an imprint of Cedar Fort, Inc., 2373 W. 700 S., Springville, UT 84663
Distributed by Cedar Fort, Inc., www.cedarfort.com

LIBRARY OF CONGRESS CATALOGING-IN-PUBLICATION DATA

Names: Stirling, Stephen J., 1953- author.
Title: Garden of the Gods / Stephen J. Stirling.
Description: Springville, Utah : Sweetwater Books, An imprint of Cedar Fort, Inc., [2016]
Identifiers: LCCN 2016030514 (print) | LCCN 2016032894 (ebook) | ISBN 9781462119387 (perfect bound : alk. paper) | ISBN 9781462127146 (epub, pdf, mobi)
Subjects: LCSH: Big game hunters--Fiction. | West (U.S.), setting. | LCGFT: Fantasy fiction. | Western fiction. | Thrillers (Fiction)
Classification: LCC PS3619.T577 G37 2016 (print) | LCC PS3619.T577 (ebook) | DDC 813/.6--dc23
LC record available at https://lccn.loc.gov/2016030514

Cover design by Priscilla Chaves
Cover design © 2016 by Cedar Fort, Inc.
Edited and typeset by Jessica Romrell

Printed in the United States of America

10 9 8 7 6 5 4 3 2 1

Printed on acid-free paper

To a loving wife, children, family, and to loving friends—all of them make life here worth living. And for a kind, gracious, and eternal Heavenly Father—who has prepared something for us to look forward to elsewhere in the ever expanding circle of life.

ENDORSEMENTS for GARDEN of the GODS

"Beginning in the uncharted territory of the Navajo Indian reservation, *Garden of the Gods* moves effortlessly through dangerous caverns and mid-century conflict. But for all of its valor, this story transcends action adventure and propels the reader into the depths of cultural identity—the hunt for a mythical beast surpassed by an even greater pursuit of faith and heritage. A timeless adventure of grit, loyalty, and tradition, *Garden of the Gods* is a book that demands attention from the first to the last page. It is a true masterpiece, and by far Stirling's best work yet."

—Brooke Passey, NY Times Bestselling Author of *The Only Pirate at the Party*

"With his signature style, Stephen J. Stirling delivers an unflinching look at man's hubris in assuming mastery over nature. What at first seems like a tale of corporate avarice gone awry quickly transforms into a harrowing adventure of being on the sharp end of nature's wrath, evoking both the wonder and horror of books like *The Land That Time Forgot* or *Journey To The Center of the Earth*. Perhaps most interesting of all, you may find yourself firmly on the side of nature as judgement is dealt out to those who deserve it most."

—Matt Carson, Author of *The Backwards Mask* and the *Black Rook-7* series

"Stirling weaves an intricate tale that transcends time and culture, bringing his readers to a place where they can ask themselves the most important questions. *Garden of the Gods* is certainly a tale of action, adventure, and vengeance; a saga of myths, men, monsters and gods. But more than that, this story is an extended parable exploring the mystery of faith."

—Adrienne Quintana, Author of *Eruption* and *Reclamation*

"In *Garden of the Gods* Stephen J. Stirling explores the timeless struggle between the mindset of faith and cynicism, the religious and the worldly. Set against the rich backdrop of Native American culture, this action-packed parable provides us with a slice of life—from a world of a prehistoric beast come to life out of legend."
    —DM Andrews, Author of *The Serpent in the Glass*

Chapter One

ETERNAL NIGHT

Darkness. Cold, silent darkness. It is almost impossible to imagine total darkness in a world where light is the master of the universe. In a darkened room, a pinprick of light always seems to seep through, driving the shadows before it. Light always finds entrance. But darkness reigned here, deep in the recesses of the mountain. This was a kingdom of eternal night. Here the shadows could run away from light, hiding in the bowels of the earth. In the caves of Oscura Mesa, disoriented by the twists and turns of a tortured earth, light had lost its way.

From somewhere far away in the black silence, a noise echoed faintly off the cavern walls. Gradually, almost imperceptibly, the echoes fragmented into blurry voices blending with the sound of footsteps fumbling along the rocky floor. And then a bare hint of radiance struggled through the dark in the distance, which finally burst around a corner in the garish beams of two flashlights chasing the darkness before them. The lights cast freakish shadows of the men who carried them, shadows that danced on the walls amidst the stalagmites of the cave.

The lead man glanced from the path at his feet to the ceiling and ducked under a low outcropping. The second man bumped his head on the overhang and erupted with a stream of profanity. The man in front looked behind him and smiled. "You gotta watch your head, Kelly."

"I'm trying to watch this needle," said Kelly, rubbing his temple. "I don't even know if this thing's working."

"Oh, it's working," the lead man reassured him. "You just keep your eye on that needle and I'll keep us on the path." He gestured to the curious square instrument in Kelly's hands, which hung by a strap from his shoulder. "But now that you mention it," he goaded, "are you sure you know how to read that gizmo?"

"If you think you can do better, Pike, you take it." Kelly thrust the device angrily at his companion with his left hand, dropping his flashlight in the process. The instrument was no bigger than a lunch box. In his right hand he held some kind of a sensor connected to the instrument by a yard-long cord. The light at Kelly's feet flickered but continued to shine.

"You'd better be careful, buddy," grinned Pike. "In this darkness that flashlight could be worth more to us than the stuff we're searching for. Now let's keep moving." Pike turned to continue down the cave as Kelly glared at him and stooped to pick up the flashlight.

But as his hand holding the sensor touched the cavern floor, a soft clicking suddenly began to rattle from the box in the darkness. Several feet away, Pike spun in place and focused on the instrument, and then on his companion. Kelly, too, looked up at Pike in amazement and then grabbed his flashlight on the ground to shine it on the device. Pike scrambled to his knees in an instant to study the gauge on the instrument. He smiled and glanced at Kelly.

Pike laughed out loud. "As they say—'Eureka.'"

Both men were on their feet in an instant. Dropping his own backpack to the floor, Pike quickly retrieved a small hammer and a chisel, while Kelly scanned the wall and marked several spots with a piece of chalk. Pike was already busy chipping away at the identified spots. The rocks from his chiseling fell to the floor as Kelly slipped them into sample bags and tucked them into Pike's backpack.

As Kelly finished his work, Pike stooped and etched a very deliberate mark on the wall, just above the cave floor. "There," Pike said, pointing to the signature with satisfaction. "To identify the sample point." Kelly strained to examine the mark and began to snicker. Beside him, his companion, joined him in the contagious humor.

Their faces made a strange comic picture, illuminated dimly by the reflected beams of their flashlights, laughing at a private joke in the dark.

"What am I missing?" A voice asked behind them in the cave. The two surveyors turned in surprise as their laughter abruptly died. A man wearing a tie and a work jacket stood before them. He leaned casually on a four-foot oak walking stick.

"Reid," Pike stood from the cave floor to face the newcomer. "I thought you were going to meet us outside the cave." Behind him Kelly was stashing his little box into a knapsack.

Reid glanced around the cave. "I figured since I had to file a report on your mineral findings that I ought to be here to see what they were. Besides," he stepped forward to examine the wall behind them, "you boys are obviously having too much fun."

"Yeah," Pike laughed nervously. "Kelly here knows some pretty good dirty jokes."

"Mm-hmm," muttered Reid as he squinted at the cave wall. "Nothing like a good off-color story to pass the time." Pike and Kelly exchanged an uneasy look as Reid set his walking stick against the wall and crouched to the floor. "Did I hear you say you found something?"

Pike knelt down on one knee and covered his chisel mark with his left hand as if to steady himself. "No, just some interesting volcanic formations." He glanced up at Kelly again.

"Well, I don't know much about that," Reid stood up. "I'm just a clerk for the Interior Department." Reaching out he felt the side of the cave with his fingers, rubbing over the chipped spots on the wall.

"We were just about to start down another tunnel," Pike interrupted nervously as he gestured further on.

Reid considered. "Then by all means let's do so. I'll even take the lead." Smiling, he snatched his staff from the wall, pointed his flashlight beam down the tunnel, and proceeded past the two surveyors. Pike and Kelly glanced again at each other, picked up their gear, and followed him.

Reid was already a few paces ahead of them as they quickened their steps to catch up. "I'd slow down a little if I were you, Mr. Reid," cautioned Pike. "This cave is pretty dangerous."

"What?" Reid let out a single laugh. "You worried about that Indian demon that protects the place?" Suddenly Reid's feet skidded in the gravel. His walking stick clattered noisily to the floor as he fell back to avoid falling into a gaping pit, which sank into the earth before them. Several rocks tumbled into the abyss and vanished beyond the reach of his flashlight beam.

Reid stared down into the hole, wide-eyed and breathless. Pike came up casually behind him and handed him a coil of rope. "No, but there are a few hundred sudden drops that could kill you."

Reid took the rope absently as he straightened to his full height. "I see what you mean. Anything down there?"

"Only one way to find out," said Kelly as he rummaged in his backpack.

"Tie that rope around your waist," instructed Pike.

Reid glanced at the rope in his hand and then at the pit as he protested. "I'm not going down there!"

"Don't be timid, Mr. Reid," answered Pike. As he did so he tied a rope around his own waist. "We're all going down there. This is how a mineral survey works. After all, you did want to come along."

Presently Kelly emerged from behind Pike with another rope, which he fastened around a large stalagmite near the mouth of the hole before throwing the remainder of the coil into the chasm. "And if it will make you feel any better," Kelly smiled blandly, "I'll go down first." He tied the other end of the coil attached to Pike around his own waist and, approaching the void, picked up the rope he'd cast into the hole.

He took one last look at Pike with resignation. "I guess you think I'm gonna hit 'pay dirt' down there."

"Well, you know what they say," said Pike, laying out the tether rope between them, "You always find the biggest apples at the end of the branch.'"

Kelly smirked and slipped his lighted flashlight into a harness at his side. "Belay me!"

4

"On belay," cried Pike as he wrapped a loop of his rope around the stalagmite.

Reid watched with interest as Kelly stepped carefully backwards, descending hand over hand and disappearing over the edge of the hole. His flashlight projected a strange array of shadows in the darkness as the sound of his footfalls echoed from the abyss. All the while the rope between Pike and Kelly unwound into the hole.

Pike gradually let out the rope he'd looped around the stalagmite. "See anything?"

"Not yet," shouted Kelly. "It's pretty deep. Must be fifty feet or so to the bottom." Pike continued to steady his companion's descent until the slack in the rope indicated the bottom below.

Pike approached the edge of the hole and called down. "Well?"

Kelly's voice was distant in the dark. "I don't see any of those big apples you were talking about."

Pike smiled. "Take a reading!" He twisted his shoulders from the cumbersome backpack he was still wearing, and hung it from the pointed stalagmite. "I'm coming down to have a look for myself." He tied the other end of the rope he'd given to Reid around his waist. "Belay me, Mr. Reid."

"Wait a minute!" echoed Kelly's voice from the chasm. "I hear something!"

Pike picked up the descent rope and smiled. "Just a bat or a mole . . . or evil spirits." He laughed at his own sarcasm as be began to let himself down the edge of the hole. Then, suddenly, he slipped, falling against the mouth of the chasm. His weight jerked Reid, rope in hand, against the stalagmite, knocking Pike's backpack to the ground. And out of the pack tumbled several sample bags, all containing rocks from the wall they'd just examined. Pike regained his footing and stared up at Reid.

Reid looked down at the pack and stooped to examine its contents. "Sample bags," he said, picking through the plastic packages, "with rocks from that last test point." He grew serious. "What is this stuff, Mr. Pike?"

"I told you, Reid. They're formation samples."

Reid was skeptical. "Seven bags of formation samples? You guys are supposed to be looking for iron ore."

Pike clambered from the edge of the hole. "All right, Mr. Reid, we were looking for iron ore." He picked up one of the bags. "And we found it. High grade hematite . . . the richest concentration I've ever seen."

"Don't give me that garbage!" snapped Reid. "I've seen enough to know that this isn't iron ore in whatever concentration."

Pike raised his left hand in protest. But as he talked, he slowly unsnapped the holster of a revolver at his hip with his right. "You can't tell a mineral like this from a sample book. Nobody expected this kind of a find on Indian land that the government is willing to give away for pennies on the dollar."

Reid was still studying one of the bags in his hand. Pike continued, "Mammoth Steel can make it worth your while to leave some of the details out of your report."

From the depths of the hole came Kelly's echoing voice, reminding them he was there. "What's going on up there?"

Pike side glanced down the pit but said nothing. Reid was considering in the silent darkness. "Maybe we can work something out," Reid finally spoke. "Tell your Mr. Webb I'd like to get together with him for a chat . . . after I have this rock of yours analyzed."

"Analyzed?" Pike's hand slid over the handle of the revolver.

"Sure," said Reid as he placed the sample into the pocket of his jacket. "If its mineral content checks out, I think we can do business." Turning from Pike, he began to untie the knot of the loop around his waist.

"Hey Pike," Kelly interrupted from below for the second time. "Help me out of here."

"Just a minute, Kelly," Pike shouted impatiently. "I'll be right with you." Drawing his revolver he took aim at Reid's back.

From the chasm, Kelly's voice was suddenly frantic. "No, I'm serious, Pike! There's something . . ." Kelly didn't finish the sentence as the sound of a piercing growl from the pit filled the silence of the cavern. Instantly the rope around Pike's waist jerked him off balance, just as he fired the gun. The shot hit Reid in the shoulder, sending him tumbling to the floor in pain.

"Pike!" screamed Kelly, now in terror. "Help me up! Get me out of here!"

Pike glanced quickly at Reid on the cavern floor and then turned to the pit. Bracing himself against the edge of the hole, he gripped the rope to help Kelly up. He drew in two quick spans when the rope yanked painfully through his fingers. Kelly's screams again echoed from the chasm but were immediately drowned by a ferocious roar erupting in the darkness.

An instant later, Pike felt himself dragged by his tether to the edge of the hole. He desperately clawed at the cave floor, while he gripped at the descent rope, which slid though his fingers. "Reid! Help me!"

Reid struggled from the ground clutching his shoulder in pain. He watched helplessly as Pike disappeared, screaming into the void, and as the tether between them vanished quickly down the hole. Grabbing at his waist, his fingers worked frantically to untie the knot that bound them together. Within seconds the rope tightened like a bowstring, snapping from his fingers and jerking him to the hole. Rolling onto his belly, he reached his hands out, grasping desperately at rocks and holes in the pocked floor, every second being dragged closer toward the terror of the pit. Hauled across the cave floor like a rag doll, he grazed against an outcropping of rock at the edge of the pit and clung to it with all his remaining strength.

Reid clenched his eyes shut as Pike's screams reverberated from below and cut off, silenced amidst another terrific roar. With that roar the rope jerked with a force that threatened to tear him in two. His fingers were losing their grip. But just as he was about to slip from his anchor, the rope snapped. His own momentum thrust him against the outcropping as the roar ceased. Panting and struggling to his feet, Reid hauled the rope quickly in from the hole. By the dim beam of his flashlight, he looked with horror at the loop that had been tied to Pike's waist, now jaggedly torn through and covered with blood.

Repulsed by the sight he drew a pocketknife and sawed fever-ishly at the rope until he cut it and threw it away from him. Then, suddenly, another fierce roar belched from the pit, this time closer. Something was coming up.

In renewed terror, Reid backed away from the hole and broke into a run. He welded his flashlight and staggered desperately through the darkness, all the while glancing fearfully behind him. Catching his foot on a rock, he fell to the cave floor, shattering his flashlight and cutting himself badly. He staggered to his feet and continued to grope forward in the darkness as a growl rumbled in the distance of the cave behind him.

Then, just as he cleared a bend in the tunnel, he saw it. Light! He could perceive the barest hint of light—the dim reflections of gray from the mouth of the cave. Without a pause, he pushed himself toward the growing brightness until daylight from the cavern entrance burst through like a beacon, perhaps 100 feet ahead. Laughing hysterically, he made his way toward the real world and life when he heard the growl behind him again, this time much closer. The smile faded from his face as he redoubled his efforts. He was almost to the sunlight when he stumbled again and collapsed to the ground. Rising up, he tripped again and fell. Clawing at the rocks, he dug his fingers into the dirt and sand on all fours, inching himself to the opening, now only a few feet away.

Suddenly the low growl rumbled just behind him. Writhing on the ground he turned and looked up as the growl erupted into a deafening roar. He opened his mouth to scream, but his terrified cries were engulfed in the rage and ferocity of that roar.

And then there was silence . . . and darkness again.

Chapter 2

THE FORSAKEN COUNTRY

According to Navajo and Hopi legend, the Vega Towachi was a land forgotten by the spirits of the universe and abandoned by the race of men. Stretching across a thousand square miles on the northeast corner of Arizona, the barren desert had once been lush and bountiful, a gift of Mother Earth and Father Sky. But the transgressions of the Old Ones—their pride, their betrayal of nature, and their rejection of the gods themselves—had been answered by the divinities with wind storms, lightning, drought, the scorching sun, and finally with the coming of the white man. Now there was nothing left of the mythical paradise but blistering heat and a parched and tortured wilderness of dunes and occasional scrub oak. Still, the isolation of this silent furnace yielded an eerie awe to the memory of the gods—stark, forbidding, and yet cloaked in hushed reverence.

From far in the distance, the solitude was broken by the whistle of a lone, timeworn steam locomotive as it labored across the vast expanse of the southwestern American desert. It pulled a coal tender and a single coach, which seemed to tax its reserves to the limit as it slogged through the heat into the lonely isolation of the scorched wilderness.

Matt Hayden twisted at his seat by the window of the passenger car. It had been a long trip—over sixteen hours—from Houston to Santa Fe. He considered the journey and smiled to himself. In spite of his long legs, he'd always been able to get comfortable anywhere. He'd actually been able to snatch a good little catnap since they'd changed trains in Santa Fe. However, the last leg of the journey across the northwest corner of New Mexico into Arizona did seem to be taking forever. Matt pulled his cowboy hat down over his face another half inch and readjusted his feet under the seat facing him. Perhaps he could doze off for just another few minutes.

He mused about the circumstances that had brought him to this point in life—doing what he loved in some of the most extreme and forbidding places on earth. It had been an unusual journey.

Born and raised in Elkhorn, Wyoming, Matt never cared much for school, though he endured an education at the insistence of his mother and the local truant officer. He would much rather have been hunting. And he was good at it.

"You've got talent," his father once told him, "Intuition."

Matt had shaken his head. He had no idea what his father was talking about.

"Intuition is . . . ," the older man struggled with the explanation. "Well, it's knowing something without thinking about it. Let's say you're hunting a deer on the run. Most of us have to make our best guess at which way he's going to turn. But you don't guess. You know. Have you ever felt that?"

Matt slowly nodded.

"You have the instinct of a hunter. That is a gift. And God gave you that gift for a reason."

But something happened one weekend when he was hunting rabbits with his buddies. He made the first effortless kill and felt pleased with himself. But when his friends bagged theirs, they each celebrated with a victory dance—like primitive hunter/gatherers bringing home venison to the starving tribe. Watching them rejoice, Matt suddenly realized something painful. He took no joy in the kill. He thought at first that perhaps he just needed bigger game. But shooting deer or elk brought him nothing but more of the same gnawing dissatisfaction.

He began going on his traditional weekend hunts only to return with nothing. Finally, in discontent, he put away his gun and gave up shooting. He grew aimless, and after he graduated from high school, a listless melancholy hung over him.

He wasn't alone. By then it was the late 1920s. The Great Depression had engulfed the entire country in a different kind of national gloom. Still, the symptoms were the same. Hopeless and floating in the wake of deflated dreams, Matt and the rest of America were cut adrift. Employment, any employment, was hard to come by. He left Elkhorn and worked wherever he could, moving from job to job. He punched steers for a ranch north of Cheyenne, rode a cattle car to the stockyards in Denver, and finally hitched a job as a roustabout for a small circus.

"I tell you what we need for this circus," he heard the boss complain one day. "We've got a worn out elephant and a toothless lion. I'd give anything for a bear."

Matt spoke up. "I'll bet I could catch you a bear."

The boss stopped and studied him for a moment. "You do that kid and I'll pay you five hundred dollars for him."

Matt left the circus the next day, hitching a train headed for Colorado. Three weeks later, he caught up with the circus in Topeka, Kansas, with a caged adolescent black bear from the Rocky Mountains. For his troubles he was given five hundred dollars cash on the barrelhead and a card of introduction to a Mr. Cochrane, general manager of the Cincinnati Zoo.

"So, you captured a black bear for the Great Western Circus," said Cochrane as he looked over the young hunter. "Very impressive. Well, listen, I'll cut to the chase, young man. I need two mountain lions, male and female, for the zoo. Of course, I don't know what kind of money Jim Pollard paid you. But we'd only be prepared to offer you fifteen hundred. I'm sorry it isn't more, but times are tough."

Matt swallowed hard, composed himself, and told Mr. Cochrane he'd be willing to make the sacrifice for a first-time customer. He spent the next month and a half in Alberta, Canada, and returned to Cincinnati with two wooden crates and two very large cats. In a surprisingly short time, there was nobody with a better reputation for collecting live animals. And more offers came with increasing frequency—and larger paychecks.

As his name spread, so did the range of his conquests. From Asia he brought back Indian elephants, Bengal tigers, leopards, and water buffalos. From Africa came panthers, rhinos, hippos, zebras, giraffes, and every imaginable wild beast in between. Within a few years his exploits became the stuff of American adventure. His name showed up in press articles, his face appeared in magazines, and his stories became the subjects of theater newsreels.

But Matt cared little for the fame. And he frankly wasn't really that entranced with the money. It was the love of the hunt that stirred his soul again, just like it did when he was a kid. The pursuit of the wild had come full circle and transcended to a higher level. This was a different kind of big game conquest.

"Desert!" grumbled the passenger sitting across from him, interrupting his musings along with any thoughts of slumber.

"What's that, Buck?" asked Matt without stirring an inch.

"I said nothing but desert," answered his restless traveling companion. He also wore a cowboy hat, perched neatly on the back of his head. "Miles and miles of desert—and sand and rocks and cactus—and Indians."

Matt lifted his hat slightly to look across the aisle a few seats up where the only other passenger was sitting. A middle-aged Native American looked lazily at the source of the careless remark without a smile and then at Hayden before turning his own attention to the stark scenery again.

"Hmm, hmm." Matt acknowledged the comment. "And you've done nothing but complain about it all ever since we left Houston."

"Well, why shouldn't I? I mean you have dragged me out to some miserable places before—from the Amazon rain forest to the frozen tundra of the Yukon. But this . . . this is by far the worst."

Matt took off his hat and leaned forward in his seat to face the man. "You know, Buck. You'll excuse me for mentioning it, but I don't recall ever begging you to come on this trip."

"Any trip," Buck corrected.

"Good point," acknowledged Matt. "In fact, considering the ray of sunshine you've been on this single train ride, I'd be hard pressed to invite you anywhere. Nobody forces you to follow me around taking your lousy pictures."

"That's where you're wrong, my friend," Buck looked at him narrowly. "I'm a slave of this," he held up a boxy, twin-lens reflex camera. "This and the public whim. There's no getting around it. The magazine-reading public loves this 'Bring 'em Back Alive' action-adventure crap of yours."

Matt smiled as he sat back in his seat. "It keeps you alive, doesn't it?"

Buck smirked and shrugged as he looked out the window again. "What did you say was the name of this wasteland?"

"The Vega To-wach-i," Matt pronounced very deliberately.

"What does it mean?"

Matt smiled again. "Vega is Spanish for fertile plain. Towachi is an old Anasazi word. It means 'garden of the gods,' or something like that.

Buck screwed up his face and winced in disbelief as the train whistle blew three times. Hayden glanced out the window, extended his arms, and stood on his feet. "Well, cheer up. It looks like you can stretch your legs now. I think we've arrived at our desert metropolis." Gathering up his luggage and a large rifle case, he walked to the car's exit as the train came to a lurching stop. Buck took a long look out the window and shook his head slowly before he heaved a deep sigh and followed.

The ancient steam engine had come to rest at a desert depot stop—little more than an Indian trading post on the Arizona Navajo Reservation. Constructed of adobe brick and corrugated tin, the depot was identified by a weather-beaten sign hanging above the door. It read, "Towachi." Boasting a limited supply of dry goods, Indian jewelry, cold beer, and Coca Cola, the Towachi depot was the bustling business center of the Tonowa Reservation. Beside the trading post, someone had parked a rusted, early 1930s model Ford truck, which was refueling from a single Texaco gas pump. And under the shade of a plywood awning sat several of Towachi's favorite sons—derelict half-breeds, too poor to eat but too proud to beg.

Three other individuals also stood at the depot stop—large men wearing working clothes and expectant faces. The moment they saw

Hayden they sprang into action. One man wearing a worn fedora stepped up to him. "Mr. Hayden?"

"Yes."

He held out his hand. "My name is Frank. I've been sent to meet you."

Hayden smiled, setting down his luggage. "Oh, well, I didn't expect . . ."

At that moment, Buck appeared at the door of the passenger car, wrestling with a suitcase and two smaller camera bags. His own camera dangled from his neck.

"No problem," answered Frank. "Boys." Instantly the other two men stepped quickly over to the platform to assist the photographer. As they did so, Frank picked up Hayden's bag. "Listen, let's help you off the train with your gear and get out of this heat. Can I take that?" He reached for the rifle case.

"No, no," Matt pulled the case in protectively. "I carry that. But there is one more duffle on the car." Frank nodded pleasantly and hurried to the carriage. Matt quickly turned in his direction. "It's in the overhead . . ."

But he cut himself short as he stood facing a young Indian woman. Pretty and serious, she stood a good seven or eight inches below his six foot frame, but glared at him with a look that would have intimidated a man of any size. Hayden was speechless. She wasn't. "Welcome to Towachi, Great White Hunter. You didn't waste much time selling out, did you?"

Hayden was completely bewildered. "Excuse me?"

"Mr. Hayden?" It was Frank. He stood beside the train with a duffle in his hand. "Would you follow me? It's not far."

Glancing defiantly at the men, the girl turned on her heels and stormed away.

As the men carried off his bags, Buck joined Matt. "Well, they seem friendly enough."

"Yeah," Matt took a quick glance at the Indian girl retreating in the opposite direction, "most of them."

"Come on," encouraged Buck and the two of them caught up with their waiting escorts. They walked a short distance to a brick structure that was new and in good repair, in contrast to the depot shack. A large banner sign across the front of the building read, "Mammoth Steel Company." Their pleasant guide pushed open the door and gestured with a casual sweep of his arm. "After you, gentlemen."

The men entered to find themselves in a spacious office. Several file cabinets lined one wall and a table stood against the other. A man in a tie and wearing glasses stood at the table, studying a set of oversized diagrams and blueprints. But he stopped to look at the two newcomers as they came in. And at the far end of the room, talking on the telephone behind a large desk sat a man in an open-collared shirt. When he saw them enter he quickly reacted. "Listen, any discussion on that new pit can wait for a few days. Someone important just arrived." He paused for a moment. "You just wait for my 'go ahead,' understand? Good."

Hanging up the phone, he stood and walked around the desk. He was stocky, of medium height, and wore a genial smile. "Well," he greeted, "you must be Matt Hayden."

"Yes," said Hayden, extending his hand. "Professor Schindler?"

"No, no, no, no," the man corrected him, while taking his hand just the same. "My name is Jeremy Webb, vice-president of Mammoth Steel." He gestured to the men who had brought them in. "You've met a few of the boys. Thank you, fellas."

Nodding, the three men set down their bags and cordially left the office. Only now did Hayden notice another huge man who had entered the room.

Webb gestured to the big newcomer. "Oh, I'd like you to meet Jim Ford, our head foreman. And this," he nodded toward the table, "is Clark Simmons of the Department of the Interior."

"It's a pleasure," acknowledged Matt. "Apparently, there's no need for me to introduce myself."

"That's a beautiful case you've got there, Mr. Hayden," said Ford with a forced friendliness. "What do you carry in it?"

Hayden gripped the case a little tighter as he glanced behind him. "A Winchester!"

This exchange was interrupted by Buck clearing his throat. "Oh," said Hayden, "this is my friend, Buck Buchannan. The piece *he* is carrying only looks less formidable." Matt turned back to Webb and assumed a more businesslike attitude. "Now, with all the formalities out of the way," he stared down Webb, "what am I doing here?"

Webb was serious and equally direct. "Exactly the question we had for you, Mr. Hayden. We went to the effort to meet you at the train because . . ."

"Frankly, Mr. Hayden," interrupted Simmons, "we're concerned about your presence in Towachi."

The muscles of Hayden's face tightened with irritation. Webb took over again, calling Simmons off with a wave of his hand. "Back off, Clark." He smiled again. "Let me explain, Mr. Hayden. For several years, Mammoth Steel has been engaged in iron ore exploration here in the Southwest. Three years ago we discovered a large deposit of iron ore on the Navajo reservation. The land happens to be rich in it. Of course it is Indian land, but there are greater issues at stake now. America has to deal with Hitler in Europe and the Japs in the Pacific. After all, there's a world war going on. So arrangements were made through the proper channels to mine here at will, despite the objections of the tribal leadership."

Matt smirked and shook his head ruefully. "That's pretty much standard procedure in dealing with the Indians."

Webb smiled casually. "National security, Mr. Hayden. You know how it is. The rights of the Indians are one thing, but not above the needs of the country and the greater good. Which brings us to the current situation." Webb turned and walked to a large map of the area on the wall. "Recently, our engineers were doing routine surveys and found a particularly plentiful concentration of ore deposits up here," he pointed to a spot on the map, "in a canyon occupied by a small native tribe called the 'Tonowa.'"

"What they found was the mother lode," Simmons broke in again. "Enough ore to supply the war effort for years. The only problem is that the Tonowa consider the canyon sacred. We made every effort to resolve the problem diplomatically, but the Indians wouldn't listen to reason. So, just last month, the federal government gave its permission for Mammoth Steel to mine the disputed area. The Tonowa have resisted violently."

Webb cleared his throat to seize the conversation again. "Recently, two of our engineers and an assistant working with Mr. Simmons were assigned to double check the survey results. They disappeared. Of course, the Indians deny knowing anything about it. And now we find that the Tonowa have brought in a hired gun. You can understand our concern."

"Hired gun!" Buck began to laugh. "Matt, these guys think you're Wyatt Earp."

But Matt was not amused. "Listen," he said, trying to be patient, "there's obviously been a misunderstanding here. I don't know anything about the Indians, their superstitions, or you. I stay out of politics and I keep clear of religion. I'm a professional hunter." He held up his rifle. "It's that simple. I pursue, trap, and occasionally bring down wild animals. And that's what I came here to do."

Behind Hayden, the big foreman let out a grunt of disgust. "Those damn Indians and that monster crap again!"

Webb was stoic. "The Tonowa have been spreading rumors about some ferocious beast running around on the reservation," he explained. "A ruse to frighten the miners and to get sympathy from the white locals. They've duped a rancher named Mike Thatcher and this Professor Schindler. And now you arrive. Everybody's all excited. Over what? A ghost story." Webb opened his hands and shrugged. "You can understand our concern."

"Well," assured Hayden, "I'm just here to do some harmless exploring. I've got no quarrel with Mammoth Steel or the federal government. So you shouldn't have anything to worry about from me."

Webb smiled and nodded. "And we don't want anything to worry about, Mr. Hayden."

From the back of the room, Ford interrupted again. "Rumor has it that that crackpot Schindler paid you a thousand dollars, sight-unseen, to come out here."

Hayden turned to him. "That's nobody's business but mine."

Webb broke in to mediate again as he walked around behind his desk. "Now, Mr. Hayden. Don't get upset. Towachi is a little spot on the map. Everybody knows everything about everybody else in a place like this. That kind of knowledge pays off sometimes—like today."

Reaching into one of his desk drawers, Webb pulled out a small stack of money and tossed it on top of his inbox. "Hayden, there's twice the money Professor Schindler promised you. And to earn it all you have to do is get back on that train and return to Houston."

Matt stood, seething for a long moment. "You're getting a little pushy, aren't you, Mr. Webb?"

"Mr. Hayden," Webb reasoned, "I'm just doing business. You've got services for sale. I'm buying them. There's nothing wrong with that."

"No," argued Hayden, "except that these services have already been sold."

"You'd be smart to take that money, Hayden." Simmons paced into the conversation, gesturing to the pile of cash.

Hayden smiled and stared him down. "Oh, would I?" He let the words hang in the air before he turned to leave. "Come on, Buck."

"Just a minute," Webb raised his voice to a near shout. This tone suited him and seemed more natural. Any pretense of friendliness had suddenly vanished. "Who do you think you're dealing with, Hayden? Mammoth Steel can crush you and your Indians like a desert beetle. We own this desert. And our law is the law of the jungle—an order of nature I think you, of all people, should understand. Survival of the most powerful, Hayden. That's us. And neither you, nor your leather-cased Winchester, nor this Tonowa demon of yours are going to stand in our way."

Webb took a deep breath. His face was hardened and his new smile hollow. "Now I'd suggest you follow Mr. Simmons advice. Take that money and clear out. Or you and you're Indians are going to find out Mammoth Steel is a lot bigger than you are. And we're not afraid of monsters."

Hayden didn't react as he shouldered his gun. "Neither am I, Mr. Webb. Excuse me."

Before Hayden even had the chance to turn toward the door, Ford grabbed him by the shoulder, and spun him around to face him. "You'd better listen, buddy." Suddenly Ford froze. Hayden still hadn't changed his expression, but in his left hand he held a large Bowie knife, poised and pointed into the foreman's stomach.

He stared at Ford. "I'm listening." With only a split second pause, Hayden threw a punch solidly into Ford's face with his free hand. As the big man toppled to the ground in shock, Hayden looked around the room, cleared his right ear with a little finger and paused with his head cocked slightly to one side. There was only silence.

"Well, if that's all, then . . ." Picking up his bags, he walked from the room.

Buck was only a heartbeat behind. Grabbing his gear and luggage, he stopped at the door and turned back to the room. "That's always been his bad ear." Nodding, he exited, closing the door behind him.

Chapter 3

THE THATCHER RANCH

Matt and Buck struggled with their bags back to the trading post, which suddenly seemed much more hospitable than the local corporate offices of Mammoth Steel. There was only a slight acknowledgment of their presence from the welcoming committee who continued to lounge in the shade of the plywood awning. Still, Hayden needed some information, and they were Towachi's only chamber of commerce.

"Gentlemen, I'm looking for the Thatcher Ranch."

"Thatcher Ranch is about ten miles up, just off the reservation," came a voice from inside the post. From the darkness stepped a weathered, middle-aged Indian in a cotton shirt and a red bandana. His black hair hung around his ears. "Did you think that big, block building was the Thatcher Ranch?" As he said it, the sprawling derelicts laughed.

"No," Hayden patiently explained. "I was misdirected." He gestured to the rusted and sunbaked old truck still parked beside the clapped-out depot. "Could I talk with the owner of this truck?"

The weathered Indian was sober faced. "You're talking to him."

"I don't know what the going taxi rate is here in Towachi, but if you can give us a ride to the Thatcher Ranch, I'll pay you five dollars."

The Indian was still stone faced as he looked at Hayden, then at Buck and back to Hayden again. He took a quick glance toward the Mammoth Steel building. "What do you think of my neighbor, Jeremy Webb?"

Hayden paused briefly. "Not much," he answered.

The Indian's hardened features gradually broke into a calm smile. "Mister, I'll take you the Thatcher Ranch for nothing."

Jim Brown Eagle piloted his vintage truck along the dirt road with the speed and careless abandon of a driver at the Indianapolis 500. Hayden sat beside him in the cab, while Buck slumped morosely looking out the open passenger window at the wan-colored desert scenery.

"My neighbor, Jeremy Webb, is like the coyote," explained the Indian as they wound their way toward the Thatcher Ranch. "He takes what he wants. He'll even kill for it. But he is a coward without the pack."

"Perhaps," agreed Hayden, "but he's got a pretty powerful pack."

"Mammoth Steel," Brown Eagle grunted. "They moved in, took over, and gutted the land. Did the Tonowa receive any payment for it or benefit from it? No. That's life on the reservation. But now they want to mine Oscura Mesa and the Canyon de Dios. It angers me."

"What makes the canyon so different?" asked Matt.

"It's sacred, and that makes all the difference in the world. It's where the Old Ones used to live. And it's where what's left of the Tonowa still live. It's where they worship."

"So, for you the issue is spiritual?"

"No," clarified Brown Eagle, "I'm not a religious man—not any more. The real life of the Indian kind of beat the religion out of me." He was quiet for a half a minute or so.

"The hold outs, the ones in the canyon, they still believe—most of 'em. They believe in the rituals and the legends—and the gods. But not me. Not the rest of us."

Jim fell silent again for several minutes. At length they rounded a hill and came to a large ranch, highlighted by a Mexican style hacienda. "Here's your stop," Brown Eagle said, breaking the silence.

But as they neared the ranch house, Hayden squinted his eyes in fascination as something caught his eye. Even Buck sat up straight as he stared in amazement. "What the heck?" exclaimed the hunter. "Could you take me over there?"

Glancing at Hayden, Jim smiled and drove the truck into the yard, past the ranch house. He stopped as Matt and Buck climbed out of the truck and stood gazing at an open expanse between the house and the corrals—occupied by a desert menagerie. Rows of sturdy cages held a broad cross section of desert wildlife—including coyotes, kit foxes, gray wolves, and bobcats as well as larger game, including a collection of mountain lions, two black bears, and a huge grizzly. The Indian grinned as he watched their fascination. Finally he spoke. "Tell you what. I'll drop off your things at the ranch house."

Hayden turned to acknowledge him. "Thanks, Jim. And thanks for the ride." He looked back at the gathered animals with keen interest. Jim smiled again at the two of them and drove off.

Buck cleared his throat. "What's going on here, Matt? This feller's got himself a wild animal show in the middle of the desert."

"Not just any show," said Matt. "Where did he get himself a grizzly?"

"This can't be a grizzly," argued Buck. "They're practically extinct. The last one in the Southwest was killed in '33."

Matt shook his head. "Well, you're looking at one." At that moment the grizzly erupted with a ferocious growl.

Buck swallowed. "Or a mighty convincing reproduction."

"Oh, he's real all right," came a drawling voice behind them. Startled they turned to see a tall man dressed in work clothes and a cowboy hat. They had no idea how long he'd been observing them. He smiled and folded his arms proudly. "Can I help you boys?"

"Yeah," said Hayden. "This is Thatcher Ranch, right?"

"Yep. You two lookin' for work?"

"Well, not really . . . ," Hayden began.

"'Cause the foreman takes care o' that. His name is Hank. He's back by the—Oh, what the heck, it'll be easier just to take you there."

As they followed him, just to be courteous, Buck struggled to break in. "But we . . ."

"Course, things are a little slow this time of year. But if you two measure up with Hank, I suppose he could use another couple of wranglers. What can you boys do?"

"Plenty," said Matt, stopping in his tracks. "Look, my name is Hayden. Is there a Professor Schindler here?"

The cowboy stopped and turned as a grin burst across his face. "He sure is. And he's gonna be awfully glad to see you. Come with me, Mr. Hayden." Leading the way, the amiable guide led them past the caged animals back toward the ranch house.

"So, 'Hunt 'em and Hold 'em Hayden,'" he said. I've was readin' about you in the *National Geographic*—about how you collect those tigers and elephants and gorillas for the big zoos."

Hayden was still curious about the menagerie. "You've got quite a zoo yourself. Pretty amazing. What's it for?"

"Oh, that?" the cowboy gestured to the lines of cages. "That's all part of the professor's work. He's a paleon . . . well, I can't pronounce it. Very scientific. He's gonna be another Darwin one of these days." He turned back to them as he climbed up the back porch to the house. "Watch your step there."

Buck stopped on the top stair to take in the panorama of the ranch. "Does Schindler own all this?"

"No," said the cowboy. "I do. Name's Mike Thatcher. Come on in."

Hayden and Buck halted momentarily and glanced at each other as Thatcher opened the door and continued inside without breaking his stride.

Mike Thatcher was a horseman by nature. Ranching was in his blood. Born in Montana to Jack-Mormon parents, he was the middle son in a passel of seven children. That meant lots of work and nothing to show for it in the tradition of his pioneer heritage. But to Mike it also meant doing what he loved sunup to sundown. He'd practically been raised in the arena.

Still, a large family had its disadvantages. The ranch was small by western standards, too small to subdivide between the four Thatcher sons. So, at the death of Old Man Thatcher, the oldest of the boys received his birthright of 120 acres of Montana open range while the other three left home to seek their fortunes.

Mike was no common wrangler though. He had a rare talent with horses and livestock. And any good foreman could see it. He wandered and worked the ranches of other cowmen from Montana to Idaho to Utah. But young Thatcher had dreams—dreams to which driving cattle and breaking mustangs were mere stepping-stones. He wanted a spread of his own. He had saved almost every penny he earned. The rest he "invested," exactly as his father had drilled into his head.

"You give a tenth of your money to the Lord," his father taught all of his children. "You'll never regret it."

"But Pa," Mike had argued, "we never go to church. Why should we give some Mormon bishop ten percent of everything we work so hard to make?"

"Son," the old man had looked him squarely in the eye, "I can't stake you to an inheritance like I wish I could. And I never gave you much religion. But this much I've learned and I pass it down to you: 'Bring ye yer tithes into the storehouse,'" he semi-quoted from the Old Testament, "'and prove me now, saith the Lord, if I will not open the windows of heaven—and shower upon you a blessing that there shall not be room enough to receive it.'" He smiled at his son. "Your mother and I haven't done badly on that promise—raising a big family on a little ranch. Now," he concluded, "you give God his due and he'll never hold out on you."

Throughout all those wandering years, Mike took his father at his word and the Bible's promise at face value. And darned if it didn't work out. He never did go to church. But wherever he was, he unfailingly sent his tithing to the nearest Mormon congregation. And like clockwork the Lord blessed him—with a bronc to break for a wealthy customer, or a horse he could purchase for a song to sell again in a month for a healthy profit.

Opportunities came like prairie wildfire. He never used banks, but the bulge under his mattress grew until he had an impressive nest egg. And when the banks failed in the 30s, he had money when most others didn't. That's when he came across an ad offering a thousand acres in northeastern Arizona—cheap.

"That's the most miserable desert in the country," a fellow wrangler reproached him as he packed his bag to go one night. "It's right on the edge of the Navajo reservation. Nobody wants that wasteland. That's why we gave it to the Indians. And they're the only company you'll have there."

Thatcher stopped. "And what's wrong with the Indians? My dad and mom taught me they were a chosen people."

The wrangler wrinkled up his face. "That's your Book of Mormon talking, Mike. Pure hogwash. Indians are nothin' but savages."

Mike turned slightly red and continued gathering his things. "I, uh, never read the Book of Mormon. But if it says the Indians are good stock, why shouldn't I believe it? None of 'em have ever done me any harm. They're nice folks."

Thatcher was determined to be a landowner. He left central Utah for Arizona the next morning, and soon the thousand acres of "miserable desert" on the edge of the reservation became the Thatcher Ranch. It wasn't much, but Mike wasn't afraid of work or a challenge—and within a few years the inhospitable spread transformed into a fine looking rancho. And it was always whispered that Mike Thatcher knew how to open the windows of heaven.

Following the rancher through the doorway of the house, Matt and Buck stepped into the large open great room of the house. The hacienda was spacious and beautiful. Animal skins were spread across the floors while mounted trophies and an occasional gun rack lined the walls. Dominating the room was a huge stuffed bear, standing in a static moment of ferocious anger, frozen in time by the taxidermist.

"Joe," shouted Thatcher. "Look who just showed up looking for you."

Only now did Hayden notice a man with graying hair and a neatly trimmed beard, smoking a pipe and pacing beside the fireplace at the far end of the room. He was deep in conversation with an old Indian wearing a high crown felt hat. But at one glimpse of Hayden, the bearded man rushed across the room. "Mr. Hayden?" he seized Matt's hand and shook it enthusiastically.

"Yes, I . . ."

"When Jim Brown Eagle dropped your bags off at the front door I couldn't believe it. I'm Joseph Schindler, and I'm happier to see you than you'll ever know."

"We were afraid you'd be working for Mammoth Steel by now," clarified Thatcher.

Buck looked at Hayden. "News certainly travels fast out here."

"Well," explained Schindler, "I talked with an Indian girl who was supposed to meet you at the train today."

Buck raised his eyebrows. "That must have been that crazy squaw who nearly bit your head off, Matt."

"She is my granddaughter," said the old Indian who had just joined the conversation with a knowing smile.

All was suddenly silent. "Oh," said Buck with embarrassment.

"Gentlemen," Matt smiled, "this is Buck Buchannan, my ambassador of good will."

"Yes," added Schindler, "and let me introduce Stone Bear, the Hawate. He's the closest thing the Tonowa have to a chief out here. You've already met Mike Thatcher."

"I've also met a Mr. Webb," Hayden came right to the point.

"Yes, I know," Schindler said in sober gratitude. "I'm glad you didn't go over to his side."

"Professor," Matt held out his hands defensively, "you might as well understand now, I don't intend to be on anyone's side. I didn't come here to fight a sacred range war."

"No, no, no Mr. Hayden," the professor reassured him. "I asked you to come here to help me capture and study a large animal. And that is precisely what I want you to do."

Hayden had been persuaded to bring his baggage into the house, though he was still uneasy about the details of his employment. Buck, on the other hand, was the perfect guest. It seemed the last thing he wanted to do was get back on the train, even if it meant a temporary stay in the southwest purgatory of the Vega Towachi.

As a matter of fact, Thatcher Ranch was a literal oasis in the Arizona desert. Matt and Buck were shown to their upstairs rooms— comfortable rancho-style accommodations, each with a soft bed and a private bath. They were both invited to splash some water in their faces and even take a nap. But Hayden was anxious to find out what this entire project was about. "Tell you what," compromised Hayden. "Let's unwind for a few minutes. Buck and I will meet you back downstairs here in, let's say, half an hour."

So it was that a short time later, Schindler waited for his guests in a relaxing book-lined study. A handful of artifacts and several dusty, open volumes cluttered an untidy desk nearby. He stood erect, absently staring at several framed diplomas and certificates on the wall. He stroked his cropped beard as he examined one of them, printed in script letters. "National Academy of Sciences," it read. "To Joseph Schindler, in recognition of contributions to the study of vertebrate paleontology." Smiling, he shook his head. *Such a big to do about nothing*, he thought.

However, Schindler's accomplishments had indeed contributed significantly to the scientific community over the past decade. Son of a prosperous industrialist in Boston, young Joseph showed little interest in the family business or the fortune to which he was entitled. Instead this intelligent prodigy sought admission to Columbia University at the age of 16—graduating cum laude, four years later with a degree in biology. Continuing his studies he further distinguished himself at the University of Chicago, where he earned his graduate degrees in botany and zoology.

At that point, young Dr. Schindler joined the faculty of Harvard as an associate professor in the department of geology and paleontology. Over the next several years Schindler earned a reputation as an accomplished researcher and instructor, becoming a full professor at the early age of thirty. Every summer he took to the deserts of North

America to apply his expertise to the accumulation of knowledge in the field of paleontology. His discoveries and collections added significant Mesozoic, Jurassic, and Paleozoic specimens to the university's Museum of Natural History—as well as others. Within five years he was asked to serve as curator and director of the museum, a position he accepted on the condition that his studies and field explorations could go on uninterrupted.

For many years, he continued to undertake his "digs" with marked success, bringing renown to the university and to himself. In many ways, his contributions had changed the way his colleagues looked at the evolutionary history of life. He did his homework, advanced his theories, and then gathered the data and evidence to prove his proposals. His expertise became the foundation of over a dozen landmark texts, printed in multiple editions, and available in the languages of three continents. The certificates papering his wall bore witness of his well-earned success and renown.

But his latest scientific conjecture had been met with surprising skepticism. The dean of his college had asked to meet with him after his first published paper on the subject. "Interesting article, Joseph," the dean had remarked, holding the current month's edition of *Journal of Natural History.*

"Thank you, David," answered Schindler. "If I'm right, we could create another whole chapter in the development of life."

"I said interesting, Joseph, not groundbreaking." Dean Andrews had dropped the journal on his desk. "Embarrassing might be more accurate."

The smile had disappeared from Schindler's face as he shook his head. "I expected a little more from you, David."

"And I from you." Dean Andrews had said, raising his voice. "The most distinguished living scholar of paleontology, and you place your own name and the name of this university in jeopardy by publishing a detailed academic paper based on ghost stories."

"But David," argued Schindler, "if those ghost stories are true, we could rewrite the prehistoric timeline."

"Indian legends, Joseph! Ancient American fairy tales!"

"Consistent across two continents," affirmed Schindler.

"You cannot base a science on folklore and bedtime stories passed down from savages," the dean said, standing his ground. "Joseph, I'm your best friend. Please drop this theory, now. Everybody will have a good laugh over it and then, with the weight of your reputation, it will all blow over. In a year they'll have forgotten about it. But if you continue to pursue this nonsense, you'll put a blot on a distinguished career that you might never put behind you."

Schindler had been quiet for a moment before he answered. "I can't drop it. Because I believe it's true. And I'll find the evidence. It's out there, David, and I'll find it."

That had been seven summers ago. He clung tenaciously to his hypothesis that the Western Hemisphere held the key to a massive shift in the prehistoric timeline as understood by the sciences of the age. And that key existed in the American West. His geological explorations gradually led him to the deserts south and west of ancient Lake Bonneville and finally to the Navajo reservation of Arizona. The answer was here, somewhere deep in these mountains. He knew it. And all that he had learned from the Tonowa confirmed his gut feelings. He felt he'd never been closer.

However, the professor's Harvard dean had made an astute prediction. Schindler's standing in the paleontological community had suffered dramatically. His classes at Harvard declined in enrollment, his most recent texts went unpublished, and his former colleagues spoke in whispers behind his back about the rise and fall of the once-respected master of natural history. And to this point he had made no concrete headway in proving his postulate. That is until recently. New evidence had come to light, and a breakthrough in his research was within reach. Now he needed this hunter from Houston to place it in his grasp.

A rap at the doorjamb interrupted Schindler's introspection. Matt Hayden stood expectantly at the study entrance.

At Schindler's invitation, both Hayden and Buck had settled themselves comfortably into chairs, which had been cleared of clutter in the untidy study. Thatcher had joined them and leaned comfortably against a bookshelf.

"Like you," explained the professor as he poured his guests a drink, "I'm a student of wild life. And though the world calls me a naturalist and you a hunter, the difference between us is negligible."

Gently prodding a house cat from a stuffed armchair, Schindler sat down and continued. "I came to the Arizona desert to 'hunt' seven years ago. But I didn't find what I was looking for until last January. I discovered it in a small valley a few miles east of here, in the northeast corner of the Tonowa reservation."

"The canyon disputed by the Indians and the miners," confirmed Hayden.

"Precisely," acknowledged Schindler. "In the wall of that canyon is a cave that sinks deep into the surrounding mountains of the Oscura Mesa. And that cave is where it dwells."

"Where what dwells?" asked Buck.

"The Tonowa call it the Nyah-Gwaheh," answered Schindler.

"The bear of the underworld," came an ominous voice from the doorway. At the entrance to the room stood Stone Bear, the old grizzled Indian they had met earlier. His skin was baked and weathered by years in the sun and his hair was long and gray under his felt hat. He wore a buckskin shirt and a simple breast piece decorated with hair pipe and small pieces of turquoise—all in contrast to his denim trousers and a pair of leather boots.

"The Hopi called him Hon Kachina," said the Indian soberly as he walked into the room. "The Zuni tribes worship him as Aincekoko. It makes no difference. He is the same."

"The Navajo and Apache also have their own names for the creature," explained Schindler, "as do other Indian nations across North America."

"Are the other names any easier to pronounce?" asked Buck.

Schindler smiled. "Ny-a Gua-hay," he enunciated very deliberately. "Accent on the first syllable of each word. Like I said, there are other names, but 'Nyah-Gwaheh' seems most descriptive. It literally means 'Great Armored Bear'—huge, man-eating, and ferocious, with a hairless hide like an elephant or a rhinoceros, making it impervious

GARDEN OF THE GODS

to attack with lances and arrows. Virtually indestructible. According to Tonowa legend, the creature sleeps for periods of a century or so and then awakens to protect and defend the people of the canyon. By the Tonowa chronology, the last appearance of the Nyah-Gwaheh was in the 1830s or '40s."

"Which means it's about ready to come out of hibernation," reasoned Matt.

"Exactly," said Schindler. "The Indians think it already has. So do I."

"That logic also conveniently explains the missing engineers," suggested Hayden.

Schindler nodded. "I know Mammoth Steel wants to blame those disappearances on the locals. However, I don't believe the Tonowa are capable of that kind of violence."

"But your monster is," said Hayden.

Schindler shrugged. "Indian myths describe the Nyah-Gwaheh as a tremendously powerful, vengeful animal."

"It is a god," interjected the Hawate. "And he has returned to punish those who have desecrated the canyon—and to restore the people to their heritage." The Hawate looked at each man in the room. "He has come again. You shall see." He paused and spoke to Schindler. "I must go. It is time for the sacrifice."

"Of course, Stone Bear," answered the professor. "We'll meet in the canyon tomorrow morning."

Nodding, the old man turned and walked purposely from the study.

The dramatic exit of the Hawate left an expectant sensation in the room. Matt stared thoughtfully through the empty doorway. Buck finally broke the silence. "Cheery personality, isn't he?"

"Don't judge him too carelessly, Buck," Thatcher defended. "Stone Bear is a good man. More medicine man than chief. There is a reason he is the Hawate. Faith is a rare commodity, even among the Tonowa. But Stone Bear is a true believer."

Hayden was anxious to get the conversation back on track. "So, this Nyah-Gwaheh is the animal you want me to capture?"

"No, Matt," quipped Buck. "You weren't listening. It's not an animal. It's not even a monster. It's a god. Heck, you're always telling me you'd like to hunt some new wild game for a change."

"That's enough, Buck!" Matt said sternly. Then he turned to Schindler. "Professor, tomorrow I've got a load of equipment coming in on a freight car from Houston. Enough equipment to catch a bear—by the description in your letter, a very large bear, or sloth, or something." He stood and crossed to Schindler's desk, setting down his drink. "Well, I can track, hunt, catch—or kill any animal you want. But I can't catch a hoax. And Professor Schindler, you've been hoaxed."

"You seem pretty sure of yourself on that score," said Thatcher.

"Yeah," confirmed Hayden, "and your Mr. Webb is pretty sure too. He thinks the Indians made up this story to frighten his miners. And I think he's right."

Schindler had been quiet for quite a few minutes. Now he stood and, stepping to his desk, picked up a large object wrapped in a white cotton towel. He turned very deliberately to Hayden. "Well, if he is right, then the Indians must have made this up too."

Leaning over the coffee table in the center of the room, Schindler unfurled the cloth bundle, spilling out its contents with noisy clatter. Each man in the room stared at the object with curious awe. There, on the tabletop, lay what appeared to be a huge gray claw, perhaps a foot long, tipped with a sharp point. Hayden stooped to observe the artifact with studious interest.

"I found this in the cavern where the Indians 'invented' their myth," said Schindler. "You tell me, Mr. Hayden. What is it?"

Hayden ran his fingers the length of the curved talon, shaking his head. "I've never seen anything like it," he finally said.

"Neither have I," Schindler confirmed. "Between the two of us, you and I must be acquainted with every living creature on the face of the earth. And this claw fits none of them."

"Maybe it's one of those fossils," ventured Buck.

"No, Mr. Buchannan," argued Schindler. "The weight alone, plus the keratin-protein composition rule that out. No, it's definitely organic."

Hayden's mind was searching for options. "What about some extinct animal. In this dry climate . . ."

Schindler shook his head. "I've had this specimen analyzed by experts at the leading universities on the West Coast using the latest dating techniques. By every estimate it can't be more than 100 years old—200 at the outside."

Hayden knelt down on one knee to stare at the claw. He was legitimately baffled. "What are you?" he asked it quietly.

Schindler looked at the bewildered hunter from the opposite side of the coffee table. "You and I can find the answer to that question together, Mr. Hayden."

The professor waited expectantly as Matt shifted his gaze to the floor.

"But there's something else bothering you," said Schindler.

"You make an interesting pitch, Professor, and your arguments are convincing. But whether this beast of yours is monster or myth isn't the only issue at stake here. In fact, the real issue walked from the room a few minutes ago," observed Matt. "If this Nyah-Gwaheh does indeed exist, are we being fair to the old man—or to the Tonowa for that matter? Are we doing the right thing?"

The room suddenly fell silent. Schindler turned to look at his friend, Thatcher.

"This is a conversation we've had before, Joe," said the rancher soberly.

"What am I missing?" asked Buck.

"You didn't miss it. You're the one who brought it up," said Matt. "To Stone Bear and the believers of the tribe, the Nyah-Gwaheh is a god. The matter is sacred. So, if this creature is for real, do they understand that we mean to lure it from that mountain and take it from them?"

Thatcher looked at the professor and shrugged as if to resume an old discussion. "You came out here looking for that thing. Now, after all these years, you've finally got it in your sights. If Mr. Hayden can find it and verify that it's there, and then if his friend here can even get some pictures of it—why can't that be enough? That was your goal from the beginning—to identify this big bear, and then study it—here, in its habitat, wasn't it?"

And it might have been that simple a few years ago," explained Schindler. "But things are much more complicated now. With Jeremy Webb and Mammoth Steel moving into that canyon, ours is a race against time and time is of the essence. That's why it was critical to bring you to the Vega Towachi now, Mr. Hayden, to show you what I've found—and to help me make a decision."

Schindler looked around at the men in the room. "I'm not sure exactly what our course will be when we find the Nyah-Gwaheh. All I know is if Webb and his men find it first, they'll exterminate it in a heartbeat. Mammoth Steel is out for nothing but profit in the Canyon de Dios. And they'll destroy anything that gets in their way."

He paused and stared at the claw on the table. "I want to save the creature."

"I'm not sure he needs saving," said Hayden as he too studied the claw.

"I don't know," Schindler threw up his hands helplessly. "One thing the Tonowa need and want is someone on their side. They want someone to stand with them. I'm willing to do that. Stone Bear and the Tonowa may not understand that reality when the dust settles. I hope they don't see it as betrayal. But they'll see the truth eventually." The professor turned to Matt directly. "Will you stand by me, Mr. Hayden?

Hayden looked up, stood, and held his hand out across the table. "Call me Matt. I've got my doubts. But if it's up there, we'll save it together."

"Good." Schindler smiled as he shook the hunter's hand. "We'll begin tomorrow."

Chapter 4

THE CAVERN AT OSCURA MESA

It was a brisk morning for the Vega Towachi—a frigid 80 degrees at seven a.m. Hayden and Buck ambled out of the ranch house, having just enjoyed the breakfast hospitality of Mike Thatcher—without the company of their hosts. Matt held his rifle in one hand and appeared agitated enough to use it. Buck, on the other hand, was as pleasant and carefree as he had been since they left Texas. "Now that was a good breakfast," he said with satisfaction as he shoved the last of a biscuit into his mouth. He carried a cup of coffee and his camera dangled around his neck.

"It was a great breakfast," acknowledged Matt, "but I didn't come here to eat."

"You're just upset because Thatcher and Schindler weren't there to greet you with morning truffles and ask you if you slept well. This isn't a five-star hotel you know."

Matt took a deep breath. "I wasn't expecting the Waldorf Astoria. But I am curious why they're not here. The cook said they left about six o'clock—without us. I want to know where they went and why they left us behind."

"They went up to the canyon," came a feminine voice from the wide front porch behind them.

Turning, they were both surprised to see the Indian girl they'd "met" the day before at the depot stop. This morning she wore a pair of denim jeans and a plaid blouse, and her hair was pulled back into a ponytail. She leaned against one of the porch supports and smiled.

"They asked me to take you up there after you'd gotten a good night's rest."

Buck swallowed and shifted on the spot. "Um, that's okay ma'am. I think a nice morning walk would do us good."

Matt smiled and stepped in. "What my friend is trying to say, is that a couple of white men might not be very good company."

The girl straightened and folded her arms as she considered. "That may be true. But then again, you never know about white men."

"Or Indians," added Matt.

The girl smiled again and stepped down off the porch. "Yah-tah-hey."

"Yah-tah-hey," answered Matt. "That's Navajo for 'hello,' Buck."

"A friendly hello," emphasized the girl. "I owe both of you an apology for yesterday. I jumped to conclusions and reacted rudely. Hardly a way to treat guests." Walking up to Matt, she held out her hand. "My name is Lilia Bluelake. Now, Mr. Hayden, if you could see your way to forgive me, I'm still going to the canyon and would be happy to give you and your friend a lift."

Hayden looked at Buck and back to Lilia. "Forgiven," he said, taking her hand. "And please, call me Matt."

Lilia sped her battered pickup truck through the dirt roads that wound the few miles to the Canyon de Dios. Matt and Buck sat in the cab next to her. The landscape was dull and forbidding. Not far away, a gust of morning wind whipped up a dust devil that danced across the gray-yellow hills.

"So why did the professor go up without us?" asked Hayden.

Lilia answered in a voice that could be heard above the grind of the engine. "He, Mike Thatcher, and my grandfather thought they'd better prepare the way for you. The Tonowa are very suspicious of any strange white men lately."

"Tell me about it. Aren't you people a little touchy about this whole thing?"

"Not when you realize what Webb's men are like." Lilia slowed the engine to take some low hills. "Ever since the miners came, they've made life difficult for my people. They burn crops, shoot cattle, and whenever they find one of our men alone, they like to shove him around or beat him senseless. They take advantage of the women too. Traditional white man 'muscle flexing' to make it clear who's in charge on the Vega—and to justify their claim to the mineral rights and now the theft of this canyon. But it's the Tonowa homeland, and the Tonowa have a right to it."

"Why don't the Indians get themselves a good lawyer?" asked Buck from the window seat.

The girl continued to stare ahead on the dusty road. "They've got one," she responded. "Me."

Lilia smiled as she considered her answer, and noted the surprised expressions on the faces of the men as they exchanged glances. Ambitious, aggressive, and independent, Lilia was, by nature, different than other Tonowa women. Her grandfather was the Hawate, the spiritual leader of the little tribe. Her father had been a member of the tribal council. All this gave her a certain standing among the Tonowa—along with a definite burden to carry. But by the time she was a teenager she was beginning to feel and resent the weight of that traditional burden. "Mother," she lashed out in frustration one day, "the life of a squaw is an endless cycle of hoeing crops, giving birth, and sweeping a dirt floor—an existence of poverty, drudgery, and submission."

"You must think my life is a terrible waste," her mother answered. She was not bitter or angry—merely matter of fact.

"I didn't say that," Lilia defended herself.

"Just remember, Little One," Mrs. Bluelake added, "this wasted life gave birth to you and spent the last fifteen years raising you— into a beautiful young woman. I take pride in you and I love you," she said with a soft smile. "And I can never think of that as a waste."

During these years of growing discontent, her father took her with him to Chinle and Window Rock on tribal business. But her visit with him to Holbrook, Arizona—and the white man's world— changed her life. For George Bluelake, it was merely a meeting with the Bureau of Indian Affairs. But for his daughter, it was her first real glimpse into a culture and way of life she never imagined.

"Is it wrong," she argued with her father, "to want to live in a house with nice furniture, to eat breakfast without wondering where lunch is coming from, to live without scratching from day to day?"

"No, my negrita," he reasoned pleasantly, "as long as you do not lose who you are in your search for what the world considers the finer things in life."

Lilia's parents were wise, gentle, and strong. But by the time she came to see it, both of them were gone, swept away by a wave of influenza that decimated the tribes. Almost every household was struck. And when it did, she and her younger brother were adopted by their grandfather—and a new life began.

Unlike Lilia, her brother, Tom, was all Indian—and an angry Indian at that. Lilia used to call it his "on the warpath" mentality. Whereas Lilia was caught up in the conflict of two divergent cultures, Tom clung to his Native American heritage with a singular tenacity that was, by Lilia's way of thinking, frustratingly simple-minded.

"I am Tonowa," was his closing argument to any discussion on culture.

"And what am I?" she countered violently. He never answered. Neither did she.

But while Tom stood by his native heritage with indignant defiance, the spiritual element of his cultural legacy was another matter. He had no need for the religion of his grandfather, or for the gods who had abandoned his people to suffer at the hands of the invading white man.

So, finding a reluctant pupil in his adopted son, Stone Bear took his granddaughter, Lilia, under his wing and taught her of the old ways and of the faith that burned in his soul. She listened and nodded and followed instructions—but it never really took. Granted, the antipathy she nurtured for the spiritual beliefs of her people was not so different from her brother's. Still, her love for the old man persuaded her to endure her training with a smile. She simply considered it a part of her broad education.

And her education is what drove her adolescent ambitions. By the time she was eighteen it was no surprise to the Hawate or anyone else that her sights were set beyond anything available on the Vega Towachi. "Grandfather," she approached Stone Bear tentatively, "I want to leave the reservation. I want to go to college."

"College?" the old man said with an expression that was supposed to resemble surprise. Then he smiled. "That is an ambition that all who know you have anticipated. Since not even a charging buffalo could stop you, you have my blessing to go. Only know that I love you, and your people need you. So, promise me you will return."

The nearest school she could afford was Northern New Mexico College in Santa Fe—and she couldn't afford that. Four years and countless sacrifices later, Lilia returned to the Vega Towachi as a college graduate—having survived the bigotry and racism of "the civilized world." She was the first of her tribe to earn an advanced diploma. But she was not greeted back as a conquering hero. "There's my sister," taunted Tom, "who went off to school to learn to be a white man." Lilia held back her tears of anger and humiliation. But in truth, the ridicule she endured from her own people was far more painful than any derision she had tolerated as a lone Indian student at Santa Fe. She'd come back to the reservation, but she hadn't really come home.

Her life was now somewhere in between. She lived again under her grandfather's roof and got a job as a teacher at the reservation school. But she really was a part of two worlds, clashing with both. It was at that critical time that she met Joseph Schindler, who'd come to the Canyon de Dios to begin his explorations and research.

But the professor's first real discovery on the Vega Towachi was Lilia Bluelake. "If it were possible," he asked her, "would you be interested in continuing your education?" By September, Lilia had been accepted to the University of Arizona, College of Law—and three years later, returned to the Vega Towachi with a degree in litigation and administration. Third in her class, she graduated with the grudging respect of her instructors—and with honors. This was all noteworthy. "After all," came the oft-repeated backhanded bigotry, "who would have expected a woman to perform so well, and an Indian woman at that?"

In spite of such generous and glowing accolades from the white world, there was still no place for Lilia to go but back to the reservation. However, this homecoming offered her a surprising reception. Waiting at the Towachi trading-post depot stood her grandfather, Professor Schindler, and Mike Thatcher. It was hardly a tickertape parade. But it was an acknowledgment, albeit small, that she had accomplished something. Stone Bear gave her a warm embrace, Thatcher offered her a room at the hacienda to hang her diploma and a place to practice law, and Schindler presented her with her first job—as a real attorney. She would never forget that day for the rest of her life.

Lilia emerged from her reverie, which had lasted only a few moments, and she smiled.

Rounding the top of the dusty hill, she continued the conversation, which was still going on. "Professor Schindler hired me on retainer to look out for the legal rights of the Indians. It's an uphill battle, but he tells me to keep on fighting. Some white men talk about the needs of the 'ill-fated' red man. The professor does something about it. He paid for my education at U of A. He built an elementary school at the crossroads south of Towachi. He even funded a small clinic in Red Rock. He's always been a friend to my people. He's the greatest man I've ever met."

"So, you believe in this big bear of his?" Hayden asked as gently as he could.

"No, I didn't say that," Lilia clarified. "Professor Schindler is a scientist. He has to look at this world objectively. I don't. I think the Nyah-Gwaheh legend is foolish. I have no sympathies for it or for any other superstition that continues to enslave the Indian people in ignorance."

She ceased to speak. The bitter tenor of her remarks left the conversation dangling awkwardly in the warm desert air. "We're coming into the canyon now."

As they came over a craggy bluff, there opened before them a large canyon, perhaps a mile in width and some two miles long. Dry, rocky, and inhospitable, the Canyon de Dios was a barren waste with few signs of life except for what appeared to be a struggling community farm on the far end of the valley. Above the small patch of yellow-green crops, clinging to the face of the sandstone wall, was carved the ruin of a small Indian village. Perched some 100 feet above the valley floor and extending to the top of the cliff, the tiny rock fortress was the only evidence of actual habitation in the sacred canyon.

Lilia stopped the pickup on the summit of the descending road and pulled on the brake. "There it is, gentlemen. All that is left of what was once a great people. The Navajo were herded into Arizona by the US Army like so many cattle. But the Tonowa have lived here in the Vega Towachi for a thousand years. Moving into the ruins of the civilization left by the Old Ones, our Tonowa ancestors made this region their homeland. They built villages, cultivated crops, planted fruit orchards on the bluffs, and worshipped their god. But as your civilization conquered the West, my civilization began to die—along with the villages, the crops, and the fruit trees. Little by little, year after year, the Tonowa were driven into this canyon. But they don't intend to be driven any further."

Shifting the truck into gear, Lilia drove down into the canyon. Descending to the valley floor, they bounced along the rocky terrain. On the way they passed teenage boys and children enjoying the cool of the morning in small groups. The vacant expanse of the canyon was their playground. "The young ones don't know yet that their life is a fantasy," lectured Lilia, "but they'll learn soon enough. They live and play here in innocence—and then gradually venture beyond the reservation to discover the world outside. That's where they meet the impassable barrier of Indian reality as they try to negotiate between the traditions of the tribe and the standards of the white culture. One way or another, the white culture wins. Some of them vanish into that world—a world that will neither tolerate them nor assimilate them.

So it ignores them. Others never venture beyond the Vega Towachi and surrender here. Those we lose to alcoholism and despair. A few of us, the lucky ones, manage to get an education with a hope of a better life. But ultimately none of us escape our heritage—a legacy of broken treaties, national neglect, and exploitation. Gentlemen, welcome to the Canyon de Dios and its proud people."

Matt strained his neck to see the approaching farm where the natives were already at work, scratching out their daily existence. Lilia glanced his way. "This farm," observed Lilia, "is the dignified effort of simple people to honor their commitment to life and each other. No federal subsidies here, Mr. Hayden. Not even grants for irrigation. What water they get they bring down in an ancient aqueduct from the mesa. Ten years ago the government built a dam on the San Juan River in New Mexico, fifty miles from here. The Indians didn't receive a drop of the diverted water. There's a proposal to build a dam east of us on the Colorado at Glen Canyon. We won't see any of that water either."

Lilia's bitter monologue accented every foot of the ride through the valley. Her invective was accompanied by the images of children with guileless smiles, young people whose faces reflected a vague restlessness, and older ones who had struggled in vain for the expectation of better things, and whose expressions bore witness to a gnawing melancholy. But there was more. They had been long disappointed by shattered hopes, but they had not abandoned them. Matt studied the otherwise impassive faces with interest. There was still something deep in the eyes of these people pushing back at despair.

The small party drove past the rows of stunted corn. Matt watched the Tonowa farmers—men and women laboring side by side among the stalks, clearing the path for the meager streams of irrigation flowing in the furrows. At best the Native American way of life here was one of survival. The few hundred families that dwelt in this canyon depended on this community farm for the necessities of life. Theirs was a subsistence economy, organized within a communal structure. They labored together, for each other. They endured and they lived.

"Lilia," Matt broke the long silence as he shook his head in bewilderment. "I hear what you're saying, but it's not what I see. These

GARDEN OF THE GODS

people should be beaten, but they don't show it. So how do they go on?"

Lilia looked at Matt and gave him a wry smile. "I've never quite understood it myself. That is what makes the Tonowa different. They embrace this suffering as part of their heritage. And with it they believe in something greater than themselves. Call it religion—call it their god. It's what binds them together, makes them responsible for each other, and gives them something to live for."

She slowed the truck as they approached the base of the canyon wall, with the Tonowa village perched high above them. She gestured to a group of younger Indians ahead. "It's the younger ones—my generation—that struggle the most. Their world is different because they know it belongs to the white man. That's their reality. They live with these facts of life without religious fantasy or superstition. That and anger. And the anger is what drives them."

Just ahead stood a small group of Tonowa young men, huddled together in a discussion. The braves looked up at Lilia coldly and resumed their conversation. "Take this bunch, for example. They're mad at everybody this morning. They may be more angry at me than you." Lilia shifted into low gear and began to grind to a halt. "I'll introduce you. But don't expect much. They've got that 'Bury My Heart at Wounded Knee' look on their faces."

She stopped beside the braves and pulled on the hand brake. All conversation suddenly ceased as they glanced at Lilia with disapproval—and eyed the newcomers with silent suspicion. Lilia stepped from the pickup truck. "Good morning, Tom," she greeted the young man who appeared to lead the other braves.

"Yah-tah-hey, sister," said Tom coldly

The brave then grew silent as Matt came up beside Lilia and offered his hand. "Hi," he said, "Matt Hayden." For a long moment Tom and the hunter engaged in an uncomfortable staring match. Slowly, without breaking eye contact, Matt withdrew his hand and reached back into the truck bed to retrieve his formidable Winchester.

At that moment, the staring match was interrupted by Schindler's voice, breaking the tension. "Matt!" the crowd parted as the professor came up to Tom and Hayden. As Schindler approached, he became instantly aware of the delicate situation. "Tom, this is the man I was telling you about."

A long pause followed but the stare and the stern expression remained. "Nice to meet you, Mr. Hayden."

The professor had done his best to extend the olive branch. He heaved a sigh. Now it was time to move on. "Come on, Matt. I've got some things to show you." He stepped away immediately, then turned and made one last offering to the Indian. "Care to join us, Tom?"

"No, thank you," he said coolly and stood his ground. Hayden glanced once at Lilia and followed the professor, Buck following him.

Lilia hardly waited for them to be out of earshot. "You didn't need to act that way, Tom. The professor has been good to us, and that man is his friend—our friend."

Tom didn't look her in the eye. "Your friend maybe. I've got too many white friends as it is." Turning, he walked away from her.

"I'm sorry about Tom," apologized the professor. "He's not alone in his resentment of the whites."

"I can hardly blame him," said Hayden. "But it isn't exactly a new issue. Abuse by idiot white men began long before the arrival of Mammoth Steel."

"True, but this time it's taken on a new complexion—here in the walls of this canyon. The Tonowa are particularly protective of this cave. It's a miracle that they're allowing me to take you into it at all."

"Their trust in you makes all the difference at this point," Hayden side glanced the professor.

"And I don't intend to betray that trust," Schindler looked back levelly.

Matt took a pause and peered up the side of the cliff, which now hung above them. He couldn't see a thing. "Oh, it's up there," said Schindler, gazing skyward. It's a shrine of nature—sacred for genera-tions. Come."

Walking to the edge of the ravine, the professor led Hayden and Buck to the steep wall of rocks, where a row of steps, barely visible to the human eye ten feet away, suddenly seemed to emerge from the rock. Schindler looked back and smiled as he began his ascent. Without a word, they continued to follow him. Matt looked up several times to locate their destination, but could still see nothing but the forbidding crags of the cliffs above. About 500 feet up the side of the valley, the stair pathway turned at a small landing and they found themselves staring at a gaping hole in the canyon wall, bounded by a huge half circle projection the size of a small corral. The flat shelf was bordered by a ledge of natural rock formations affording it perfect shielding from below. And at the center of the shelf were a pit and an altar, both of ancient construction.

At the edge of the altar, basking in the shade still afforded by the overhead cliffs, waited Mike Thatcher, whittling on a stick. Stone Bear, the Hawate, stood nearby. But Matt barely acknowledged either of them, standing in awe as Buck caught up with him. "This is incredible!" he said with awe as he surveyed the ledge where they stood. "You can't even see this shelf from the canyon floor. And look at it," he gestured to the lip of rock surrounding the periphery of the shelf. "This rim offers the perfect defense from attack."

Schindler half smiled with disappointment and shook his head. "That was its last practical use. This is where the Navajo holdouts made their stand against the Federal Army in 1863. Unable to root them out, the army finally laid siege. On the verge of starvation, one hundred and fifty men finally surrendered and made the Long Walk with the rest of their people to eastern New Mexico. The rest is sad history."

"What's the Long Walk?" asked Buck.

"The three hundred mile forced march across New Mexico, Buck," said Thatcher. "On the trail and at Bosque Redondo hundreds of the Navajo people died of malnutrition, exposure, starvation, and disease. Today we call it government assistance."

"So much for the perfect protection," commented Matt.

The professor nodded. "That's because it was never intended as a place of military fortification, but as a place of worship. It's hidden from the floor of the canyon not just to keep it safe, but also to keep it sacred. The Tonowa told the braves not to make their defense here. The warriors ignored them and the result was disaster."

Matt and Buck said nothing. Then Stone Bear spoke. "The Navajo braves never would have survived here. Not with one hundred and fifty. Not with one thousand and fifty. They had guns. But they had long abandoned their faith. So they were abandoned by their god— the god that was behind them in the cave." The Hawate turned and looked into the darkness of the cavern entrance.

Buck swallowed hard. "Weren't the Tonowa driven out as well?"

"Yes, with the Navajo," said Schindler. "But eventually they were all allowed to return to the reservation, which included parts of their homelands. The Tonowa came back to this dusty canyon to watch over it."

Matt stepped over to the altar where Thatcher was still leaning. "So the Tonowa built all this?"

"No," said Stone Bear, joining the conversation again. "This altar was built by the Old Ones, hundreds and hundreds of years ago. We are merely the caretakers of it. So it is that every night, my people leave an offering on this altar to their god." The Hawate paused and looked intently at the white men. "And every morning it is gone." His expression remained serious. "Shall we go inside?"

Without waiting for an answer, the old man climbed to the mouth of the cave and stood.

"Well, Mike?" Schindler said turning to Thatcher.

"You go on," he held up his hand apologetically. "I've broken wild mustangs and I've sat atop a ragin' bull—but I don't do caves." Schindler shrugged and stepped up to and into the cave, past Stone Bear.

But as Hayden tipped his head forward to follow the professor, Stone Bear stopped him. Taking him by the shoulders, the old Indian, stared up into his eyes studying him. Matt was transfixed as he looked into that leather-hard face—a face worn into a thousand tiny wrinkles. The Hawate finally spoke. "Before you enter, I must know one thing. Are you pure in heart?"

Matt was momentarily stunned. Suddenly he felt dwarfed by the old Indian. It was like being summoned in to see the Mother Superior at his old Catholic elementary school. The look in the Hawate's eyes was the same. It was a look you couldn't lie to. "Pure in heart"? Was that the price of admission into the cave? He couldn't answer that. Life had taught him that no one was pure in heart. It was the 1940s. War threatened to destroy the world. He was living in a generation hanging on by their fingernails. Nobody was that clean in this day and age. He was honest, he supposed. But more than that he could not claim. He opened his mouth to speak, but nothing came out.

Then all at once, the Hawate's hardened features softened. He somehow understood. Without torturing Matt for another second more, he asked another question. It was, Matt knew, a merciful rephrasing of the first inquiry. "Mr. Hayden, are your intentions true?" Matt searched his thoughts. Why was he here? Why did he want to enter that cave? And why did he want that creature to be real? And in an instant he knew it was more than another glorious capture, more than the adventure of a lifetime, and more even than his anger at the arrogance of Mammoth Steel. He wanted this people to have something. Perhaps they would not be justified by the existence of a god—but he wanted them to be vindicated in the reality of their creature in this mountain.

"Yes," he said.

The Hawate nodded with a barely perceptible smile as he released Matt from his grip and his stare. He turned and walked into the cavern.

"Come on, Buck,"

"Uh, no thanks," answered Buck, who had been watching Hayden's rite of passage. "I'm not sure I'd pass the 'entrance exam.'" He took a seat on the altar. "I think I'll wait out here with Thatcher."

"Suit yourself," Matt smiled. "But remember, you're sitting on a sacrificial altar." He disappeared into the cavern.

Buck quickly stood to his feet. "Mike?" he asked with concern. "This thing's already been fed, hasn't it?"

Saying nothing, Thatcher simply smiled as he continued to whittle.

In the dim shades of reflected sunlight, Hayden tried to adjust his eyes to the shadows of the cave. As several seconds elapsed, the shadows gradually dispelled and he found himself standing in a spacious cavern, roughly ten feet in diameter. Though scored with thousands of pock marks, it was surprisingly clear—unobstructed by rock formations or outcroppings. He looked into the depth of the cave where the light was swallowed up in the blackness. Turning to look at the walls he watched a pattern slowly emerge from the volcanic rock. As he squinted, a hundred ghostly handprints came into focus—the signatures of the earliest occupants of the canyon and the first caretakers of the cavern. Suddenly, Schindler stood beside him. "Those handprints are thousands of years old."

"Professor," asked Matt, "who are the Old Ones?"

Schindler shook his head. "The Anasazi, we think. Too far back to tell for sure. This cave is ancient." The professor held up a kerosene lantern and handed it to Hayden. "Here, you're going to need this."

Hayden took the lantern and looked at it. "Don't you have flashlights?"

Sshindler sighed. "Electrically generated illumination is 'polluted light,' they say. The Tonowa are old fashioned, at least about the cavern. They prefer the fire to artificial light in here—out of respect to the gods."

"Naturally," said Matt, taking the lantern. "Where's Stone Bear?"

"He's gone up ahead," said Schindler, ". . . without a lantern. He never seems to need one." Schindler turned toward the darkness, holding his own lamp high. "Follow me and watch your step."

Without another word they began to move down the cave. But the silence was only momentary. "How far into the mountain does this cavern go?" asked Matt.

"In one sense it goes on forever," answered Schindler. "This entire canyon is a labyrinth of volcanic fissures, lacing the surrounding mountains—perhaps as far as the San Juan River. But above the level of the water, I've found only this one entrance."

"Or exit," pointed out Hayden.

"True." The professor stopped mid-step and pointed to the ground. "Here's something you'll find interesting."

Shining his lantern low over the cavern floor, Hayden stooped down to examine a strange set of tracks at their feet. His mouth fell open as he peered at one huge paw print more closely. Glancing up at the professor, he studied the track again, shaking his head.

"What do you make of it?" asked Schindler expectantly.

"It's a bear print—sort of." He reached out to the end of the toe indentations and the soil where something was missing. "But where are the claw points?"

Schindler nodded his head. "He's adapted to the rocky terrain of his environment. I believe they retract and extend according to need. That protection also keeps them razor sharp."

"Professor," noted Hayden. "With a footprint of thirty-five inches, this bear of yours is going to stand over twenty feet tall." He looked around at the cave diameter. "This cave is big by any standard. But would our friend have enough space to maneuver here?"

"Remember, he's also got the eyesight of a cat as well as the hide of a rhinoceros," said Schindler. "He's doubtless adapted in a few ways down here."

Schindler stood and continued. Hayden lingered for a moment to look once more at the tracks and then hurried to catch up with his guide. Navigating his way through the cave by lantern light another hundred feet or so, he finally stopped when he came to the professor and Stone Bear waiting at a huge wall of the cave. The Hawate held up his hand for Hayden to halt. "This is as far as we can go."

Hayden had thought they would be going deeper, but didn't argue with the stern expression on the old Indian's face. In answer, Stone Bear lifted his lantern, illuminating the cavern wall behind him to reveal a large face painted in fading colors. The totem wore an appearance of terror through eyes that still stared at Hayden after a thousand years.

"It's kind of an ancient Indian stop sign," explained Schindler, "forbidding the feet of man to pass beyond this point. That's the only part I need to translate. The rest is pretty clear."

Glancing at the professor, Hayden held his lamp over his head. The light splashed across an ancient tableau of images and petroglyphs extending several feet along the cave wall. Vultures circled in the air and other scavengers followed them on the ground. Figures of men retreated and scattered in frightening disarray. And dominating the picture stood a massive and muscular hairless bear–like creature with large claws and a gaping jaw. It stood towering over its prey, holding an elk in one hand and a man in the other. Beneath the paining was inscribed a series of primeval characters. "This writing underneath," asked Matt. "What does it mean?"

Stone Bear answered him. "Let no man violate the sanctity of this cavern, or the people of this canyon—or they will face the vengeance of the Nyah-Gwaheh."

Chapter 5

THE INVASION OF THE CANYON

Suddenly the three of them were brought back to reality by the echo of gunshots coming from the world outside the cave. The professor and Hayden looked at each other for a split second, before turning to run toward the single exit to the canyon. Matt arrived at the mouth of the cavern first. The moment he did a bullet ricocheted off the rock above his head. Instinctively he ducked for cover, back into the shelter of the cave.

"What is it?" asked Schindler as he arrived beside him.

"I'm not sure," said Hayden, leaping from the cave mouth to the protection of the shelf below. There, positioned around the rim of the ledge, Tom Running Wolf and several other Indians had fortified the sacrificial landing as they fired their guns at the canyon floor below. Hayden crouched beside Tom, mechanically cocking his rifle amidst the shower of bullets. Tom glanced at him quickly as he took another shot over the rim of the ledge. "Welcome to the battle, Hayden. Make yourself useful."

Poising himself at the edge, Hayden peered carefully over the top for a view of the valley floor below. At the foot of the canyon wall he could see a group of federal marshal vehicles arranged in a defensive position, with several deputies taking cover behind them.

Another bullet struck the ledge, so close to Hayden that the dust from the impact sprinkled onto his head. He jerked back for cover when he heard a voice over a bullhorn echoing above the din of gunfire. "Hold your fire! Hold your fire! This is Clark Simmons of the Department of the Interior."

As the volley of bullets stopped, Hayden peered again over the lip of the ledge in the direction of the voice. Even from this height, he recognized the bespectacled Simmons, hunkered down for protection, bullhorn in hand, behind the front door of one of the marshal's vehicles. Simmons stood. "You people are occupying government land illegally. You must leave these premises without delay in order for mining operations to progress unimpeded. Federal representatives will provide you with transport, tents, bedding, and food if necessary until you can be relocated permanently."

Hayden shook his head in disgust as he sunk down, leaning against the short wall of protection. Mammoth Steel had wasted no time in robbing the Tonowa of the last of their heritage. Exhaling with a grunt, he turned his head to see Tom, studying him with interest. The Indian smiled bitterly.

Below them on the ground Simmons continued. "However, you must leave immediately. I repeat, you must cease resistance and leave these premises immediately." As he listened, Tom's jaw tightened in defiance. Standing, he fired. Simmons dropped the bullhorn to the ground and ducked again behind the car door. The shooting instantly resumed.

At that moment a lone figure stepped from the cover of a pickup truck, positioned out of the line of fire beyond the marshal's vehicles. Lilia Bluelake had seen enough. Resolutely she walked through the gauntlet of cars and gunfire. She stopped briefly at the car where the marshal and Simmons shielded themselves against the violence. Looking down at the cowering official, she reached down and picked up the bullhorn, before she continued to walk toward the canyon wall.

The marshal stopped shooting and watched with interest before he held up his hand. "Hold your fire!" he shouted. Gradually, one by one, his own deputies ceased to discharge their weapons.

"What are you doing?" shouted Simmons.

The marshal answered with a glance. "I said, hold your fire," he repeated and continued to watch the Indian girl.

The braves at the ledge of the cave platform continued to shoot however. Though careful to not endanger one of their own, their anger had been ignited. But Lilia was not to be ignored. She stopped in front of the law enforcement vehicles and held up the horn. "Stop shooting!" She waited and repeated again, "Stop shooting, now!" Suddenly it was quiet. "This isn't the answer. You're not going to solve anything by killing the marshal and his deputies—or yourselves."

Perched on the canyon ledge outside the cave, Matt, Tom, and the others listened to Lilia's plea. "There are still legal remedies. Please, just give the law a chance."

Matt watched Tom as he struggled with Lilia's words in the lull. Beyond the rim of the ledge, the slamming of car doors and the tumult of men in motion could be heard. The martial and his deputies were coming.

"She is right, Tom Running Wolf." The words came from behind the defenders of the sacred shelf. Tom turned to see the Hawate and Professor Schindler standing at the cave entrance. The old man stepped from the opening and walked to where the brave still crouched on the ground. He rose to his feet as Stone Bear stopped in front of him. "My grandson," he said, "you cannot fight these men with guns."

Slowly Tom set down his rifle, but his eyes were still full of bitterness as he stared past the Hawate into the blackness of the cave. As he did so, several of the marshal's men climbed over the short wall onto the ledge, immediately disarming the braves.

"Matt!" It was the voice of the professor as he knelt beside the altar. "It's Buck." Leaping to the altar, Matt arrived in time to help Schindler lift his friend to a sitting position in the sacrificial pit. Buck was groggy, but alive. Up to this moment Hayden had been oblivious to everything but the stand-off on the ledge.

"Have you been shot, buddy?"

"No," said Buck, blinking his eyes. "Just whacked in the head when the excitement began."

"Where's Mike Thatcher?" asked Schindler.

Buck was still rubbing his head trying to think clearly. "He went down the hill when the MPs arrived. Wish I had."

"Listen," Schindler stood, "I'd better get down there and find out what's going on." He left without another word.

Taking Buck by the arm, Hayden began to lift him. "Can you stand up, pal?"

"Yeah," Buck said, struggling to his feet. "I was just stunned a little, that's all."

Matt leaned on his rifle, and held Buck up with his other arm as one of the marshal's deputies approached him roughly. "I'll take that rifle, mister."

Hayden bristled as he put both his hands on the Winchester. "No you won't."

"He wasn't involved, deputy," defended Buck. "Ask any of these men."

The deputy drew his pistol. "I said, I'll take that rifle."

"Deputy," a voice interrupted the confrontation. It was Jeremy Webb. He stood at the rim of the ledge, smiling as he surveyed the situation. "There's no reason to arrest that man or take his weapon. He's just out looking for Bigfoot." He burst into a booming laughter and walked away.

Down on the canyon floor, trucks and equipment from Mammoth Steel were already moving onto the land, while at the same time, Indians were being forcibly escorted in the opposite direction. Women wept as they herded their children around them. Husbands followed close behind, wearing empty expressions on their faces. They and their ancestors had been through this before.

In the center of it all stood the marshal, watching the scene in dismay as he talked with Clark Simmons—the representative of the federal government.

"You indicated you'd have some means of moving them out," observed the marshal.

"Yeah," shrugged Simmons. "Well, that didn't work out. What difference does it make? The Indians have been walking for thousands of years. All you have to worry about is getting the rest of those

Tonowa out of that cliff village on the wall of the canyon. There can't be more than one or two hundred of them up there."

"And those tents and other provisions?"

Simmons side glanced at the marshal. "They'll be there in a couple of days—maybe."

He turned and began to walk away when he came face to face with Stone Bear. "Mr. Simmons."

Simmons was more than a little put out by another interruption. "Yes," he said impatiently.

"We are complying with the law and cooperating with authority."

"Listen," said Simmons, looking around, "I'm pretty busy."

Grabbing Simmons by the shoulders, the Hawate grasped his attention. "What I have to say is important." The government agent was momentarily his silent audience. "We intend to obey your wishes. But we must be allowed to return to offer sacrifice—tonight."

Stone Bear continued to hold him in a powerful stare. But in an instant the spell was broken. He licked his lips and fumbled for words. "Sacrifice?" he said dully. Shaking his head, he smiled at the absurdity of the request. "No, old man," he said emphatically. "I'm afraid that's totally out of the question. You're going to practice these rituals elsewhere. This canyon is not your home anymore."

Backing away from the old man, he finally turned and began shouting orders again. "Okay, start them walking out of the canyon to the south!" He left the Hawate in silent thought, looking up the canyon wall to the cave.

Mike Thatcher walked amidst the confusion, trying to restore some order among the Indians. "Mike!" he heard a man's voice. He turned to see Lilia and Schindler weaving their way through the crowd toward him.

The rancher stopped, crestfallen as they came up to him. "This business really stinks, Joe. Hundreds of people driven from their homes like a herd of buffalo."

"Mike," pleaded Lilia, "they've got no place to go."

"You know better than that," Thatcher put a hand on her shoulder. "I've been tryin' to spread the word. Tell the tribe they can squat on the grazing land south of the ranch 'til the dust here settles."

"Thanks, Mike," she said.

"In the meantime, Lilia, what can be done about this?" Mike asked.

"Well," she explained, "first I'm going to town to get my brother and the others out of jail. Then maybe a higher court can restore them to the canyon again. I don't know."

Schindler took her by the arms in a fatherly embrace. "I'm proud I was able to help you through law school. You have a destiny with this people. Now, you'd better hurry."

"Come on, Lilia," invited Thatcher. "Maybe I can help you parley with the marshal in town."

As they turned to leave, Hayden and Buck approached them. "Professor, Mike," said Matt. Then he paused as he looked at the Indian girl. "Lilia, I'm so sorry about this."

"Thanks, Matt." With only a pause she turned to Thatcher. "Let's see what we can do, Mike."

She then hurried off, practically leaving the rancher behind. The others watched as they disappeared into the sea of exiled Tonowa.

"That's a brave girl," said Schindler, almost more to himself than to the others. Then he gazed around. "This is a brave and longsuffering people. For them," he looked again to Hayden and Buck, "it's a familiar story. So, history repeats itself, even on the Vega Towachi." Turning, he began to walk.

Matt and Buck followed. "I guess I shouldn't be surprised. But I admit, I'm disappointed. I'm sorry it had to end like this, Professor."

"End?" Schindler said as he stopped abruptly.

Matt was straightforward. "Professor, your hunting expedition is over." Exasperated, Schindler continued to walk and Hayden followed after him. "I realize you couldn't have foreseen any of this. I'm releasing you from your contract. I'll be giving back your deposit too."

Arriving at his flatbed truck, Schindler turned on Hayden. "So, you're quitting?"

"I don't see that any of us have a choice," argued Hayden. "There's sure not much hope of us getting into that cave now."

"On the contrary, Matt, we've got every hope—and I've got every intention to go deep into that cave—and to capture and study whatever's inside." He looked squarely at Hayden. "I've been working on this project for seven years. Too long to let something like this stop me." He was fervent now. "See this through with me, Matt. I promise you, you're going to claim the catch of the century in there."

Hayden had been listening with mixed emotions. He was a pragmatist by nature. But he was also a hunter. He wanted to know. He wanted the Nyah Gwaheh to be real. He glanced at Buck, who was still rubbing his head.

"Don't ask me to help you make this decision. You already know what I think." He took a panoramic view of the canyon. "Wild horses couldn't drag me away from this paradise."

Hayden took a deep breath and exhaled, shaking his head. "OK. Listen, Buck is still a little punchy. Why don't you take him back to the ranch with you. Meanwhile, I'll get down to the whistle stop and get my heavy equipment off today's train."

"Sure," said Schindler, smiling with satisfaction. "Take Thatcher's horse hitched to the back of my truck."

Matt nodded and walked to the bay mare tied to the rear bumper of the professor's flatbed. Taking the reins, he swung himself up into the saddle. Schindler continued. "Is there anything else I can do?"

"Well, yes," said Hayden as he controlled the animal. "See if Thatcher can send a few hands and a trailer to the depot in a couple of hours. I'm afraid this shipment won't fit in the saddle bags."

"The men will be there. I'll see to it, myself," said Schindler, climbing into the truck.

Buck pulled himself into the passenger seat as Matt sidled up beside the truck. "You gonna be okay, buddy?" he asked.

"Yeah," Buck sighed. "I'll hold down things at the ranch. See you this afternoon."

Matt smiled and began to turn his horse when Schindler spoke. "Thanks, Matt. You won't be disappointed."

"Let's hope none of us are, Professor." Gently nudging the mare with his heels, Hayden rode away in the direction of the Towachi depot.

The shades of evening were already closing upon the desert by the time Lilia, Thatcher, and Tom Running Wolf returned to the ranch. Long tendrils of pink and orange clouds stretched across the southwestern sky, reflecting the last rays of the day's light. Lilia drove the pickup to the front porch of the ranch house and stopped. Thatcher, sitting in the front seat, climbed out the passenger side.

"Sorry the tribe has to sleep out under the stars tonight, Tom," Thatcher said as he slammed the door shut behind him.

Tom, sitting in the center of the cab, heaved a deep expressionless sigh. "It's fine," he said. "The stars are the only thing the white man can't take away."

Thatcher looked at Tom for a short moment before he responded. "You know, Tom, you could just say 'thanks.'" He waited in the twilight. Tom's only response was silence as he stared blankly ahead. Thatcher gave a wry half smile and gently patted Tom on the shoulder. "What a nightmare of a day. Stop at the bunk house and have the foreman give you some more bedding and blankets to take back to camp. Good night."

As Thatcher walked off, Lilia opened her door and got out. "Take the truck, Tom," she said as she closed the door. "Bring it back in the morning. Maybe we can start discussing what's next for the Tonowa."

"What's next?" asked Tom incredulously. "What's left?"

"Tom," she faced him frankly, "we might not get the canyon back. But we've got to live somewhere and we'd better start planning on it."

"Lilia," his dark features turned on her unapologetically. "Have you given your heart so much to the world that losing your heritage means nothing to you?"

Lilia didn't need to consider. Her answer was instantaneous. "We lost our heritage a long time ago, Tom. I just recognized it sooner than you did." Turning her back on Tom and the pickup, she walked to the house. Behind her, the truck engine cranked alive and the sound of it faded into the distance as Tom drove off. But Lilia hardly heard it. Already lost in thought, she was not half as cynical as she pretended to be. Dejected by the day's events, she entered the ranch house and closed the door behind her. She leaned against it and shut her eyes. With a deep breath she forced her feet to move across the room and began to climb the stairs.

"Lilia!" called the voice of the professor. "I'm glad you're back. I've got to talk with the Hawate. Did he return with you or is he back at the encampment?"

She stopped at the landing. She was exhausted. "I suppose he's with the rest of the tribe. Haven't you looked there?"

"Well, earlier, yes," said Schindler. "I finally assumed you were still getting him out of jail."

She turned on the stairway, her hand still on the railing. "Grandfather wasn't arrested."

"Then where is he?" asked the professor.

Pausing only briefly, Lilia ran down the stairs and headed for the door.

"What is it, Lilia?" Schindler asked.

She didn't stop to explain. "Tell Mike I've taken one of his horses."

"But where are you going?"

Stopping, she turned at the door. "The canyon—to find Stone Bear." Then she was gone.

Chapter 6

VENGEANCE FROM THE EARTH

A campfire burned on the floor of the Canyon de Dios amidst trucks and mining equipment. It had been a busy day for Mammoth Steel. But other than some ambitious preparations for the work of excavation, no actual mining had taken place on the day of invasion. The objective of Jeremy Webb on this first day had been simple and reduced to one word: occupy. Hence, day two would be the beginning of demolitions—and the blasphemous violation of Oscura Mesa. Most of the mineworkers had returned to their base camp nearby to get a good night's sleep. Only a token contingent had been left in the canyon to defend it and watch over the equipment. The mass of Mammoth's might would return in the morning to begin the real work.

The three miners on security detail huddled around the small fire. Two of them, Hicks and Maddox, were grunts at the low end of the employment food chain. Guard duty was their curse for the evening, and they were getting good and drunk in retaliation for it. The third man, Ford assigned himself to the detail, hoping against hope that an errant Tonowa might return and allow him the opportunity to exercise a cruelty he'd already excelled at—this time in the name of the law. Ford stayed sober, in anticipation of a night of vicious pleasure.

Hicks was already well on his way to a drunken oblivion, announcing his frustrations with loud and loquacious profanity. "I was gonna be the first to sink my pick axe into that mountain. Leave my mark on the son of a . . ," His voice trailed off. He shook his head as if to rattle life into his gray matter again. "Supposed to be a deposit in there like nobody's ever seen before." Ford sat nearby. A droll smile passed across his face.

"A miner takes pride in a thing like that," Hicks rambled on. "Like drawing first blood. After staying up here all night, I probably won't even be awake for the first blast."

"What are you complaining about?" bellowed Ford. You're getting paid double time for your 'vigilant' guard duty. That's more than you're worth."

Maddox was standing morosely by the fire. He was a little less drunk than Hicks—but not by much. "I'm not complaining," he slurred. "I need the money. Besides," he emphasized his words with a sarcastic effect, "somebody had to stay and protect the precious company equipment. Leave it here, unattended for the night, and one of those savage Indian raiding parties might come and carry it all off."

There was a pause before they all burst into laughter. Even the cheerless Ford chuckled. "Personally," he said, "I wish some of those Indians were around tonight. It might be nice to have the company of a little squaw or two to keep me warm."

They all laughed again.

While the laughter continued in the valley below, a lone figure struggled up the measured steps carved into the canyon wall. Stone Bear paused in his exertions, and he straightened to look in the direction of the profane amusement as a light breeze carried the mirth in another direction.

It was a long climb up the steps to the ledge. Several minutes went by as he renewed his labors up the stairway. He strained again to see the men around the campfire, but he could only make out the flicker of the blaze. The dying fire gave him a sense of direction in the darkness. Leaning over, he resumed his work and strained at his burden, a large deer, which he was dragging up the canyon wall. The Hawate had a rite to perform—a sacrifice of devotion to his god.

He pulled with all his might, one agonizing step after another, up the cliff. He almost lost his balance at the switchback, falling to one knee before he righted himself and hauled the beast, painfully, foot by foot to the brink of the ledge. Straining himself with his last ounce of energy, he shoved the animal over the final obstacle, and then inched himself onto the flat, where he tumbled to the ground and slumped down by the edge of the sacrificial pit, panting in exhaustion.

Suddenly the voice of Ford laughed behind him. "Well, men, looks like we have a visitor." The Hawate turned to see the foreman looming over him.

Beside Ford swayed a half-drunken Maddox. "And he brought along a little midnight snack—for somebody."

Behind them, bracing himself against the mountain side, stood the inebriated Hicks, wielding his pick axe. Oblivious to all else, he swung back the axe and sunk it deep into the canyon wall. "There!" he grunted with satisfaction. "First blood!"

Ford took one step toward the frightened old man with a cruel smile on his face. "Just what I was thinking." Without a pause, he struck Stone Bear with all of his strength.

Hayden burst out of the ranch house door carrying his gun, followed by Thatcher and the professor. "Well, why didn't you try to stop her?"

"Stop Lilia?" questioned Schindler. "It's like stopping a windstorm."

Hayden dropped his rifle into the saddle holster and climbed onto the horse. "I'll need this horse again, Mike. Meanwhile have your boys take the smaller firearms and rounds into the house. Leave the larger equipment out here."

"Shouldn't some of us go with you?" asked Thatcher.

"No," shouted Matt. "But get ahold of Webb. Tell him if anything happens to that girl, I can use this stuff on him as easily as I can on your big bear." Reining the bay around, Hayden rode off in the direction of the Canyon de Dios.

The canyon was quiet now, bathed in the chill night by a consistent breeze that seemed to engulf every sound in the darkness. A pair of boots walked up the stairway carved into the mountain. Lilia was carefully making her way up the canyon wall when she began to hear voices. Taking cover off the stair-stepped path, she waited until three men passed her. They walked so close she could have touched them. Two of them were carrying something.

"Don't you think you were a little rough, Ford?" asked one of them.

"Shut up," came the gruff voice of the one walking in front. "We've got a job to protect the place, don't we?"

"Yeah, but . . ."

"Then shut your trap," threatened the leader again.

"This thing's heavy, Ford," slurred the third man, speaking for the first time.

"Well, get rid of it then," said the man called Ford. "It's a straight drop from here."

Peering into the darkness, Lilia strained to see what they were dropping off the ledge. With a grunt, the two men heaved something over the brink. In the backdrop of the sky, lighted by a half moon, Lilia saw the distorted silhouette of a body disappear into the darkness. She let out an involuntary gasp as the three men turned toward the black crags of the mountain.

"What was that?" said Ford.

"Maybe it was the deer," slurred the drunkard.

"Idiot!" shouted Ford. "It was over here." He took one footstep in Lilia's direction, almost stepping on her.

The first man grabbed the foreman by the arm. "Ford, let's just get off the mountain. This place gives me the creeps."

A gust of wind was all that was needed to persuade the big man. "Yeah," he said. "We've done what we came to do here. So much for feeding time."

In a moment the men had all quickly retreated beyond the switchback and were gone. Lilia crept from her hiding place against the rocks in the darkness and crouched low as to not be seen. She looked up in the moonlight toward the mouth of the cave and listened as the wind died down. Not far from her, off the path of stairs, she heard a moan. Leaving the steps she felt her way up the cliff wall to a cleft in the mountain. She peered among the rocks as the faint, intermittent groaning continued. Then she saw something. A hand. Scrambling to it, she reached down and lifted her grandfather from the cleft. He turned his face skyward, but lost his strength and fell again. Bruises and dirt covered his face, and blood trickled from a huge gash in his gray-haired scalp.

"Grandfather!" she cried, trying to sit him up. In vain, he tried to speak but was too weak.

Suddenly, a figure loomed up in the shadows behind them. Lilia started to scream when a hand covered her mouth. "It's me," whispered Hayden. Instantly he released her and leaped down to help. "How bad is he?"

"He's dead," she whispered somberly.

"No," said Matt, appraising his wounds as he held a hand to the old man's neck. "But I'm surprised he's not." He took a quick look at the campfire below them. "It makes me want to kill somebody."

At this Stone Bear stirred. "No!" The old man struggled to speak. "Atalabo doroba."

Matt looked at Lilia. "It is the old tongue," she said. "'Atalabo doroba.' It means, 'Vengeance is mine.'"

"Tell him not to talk," said Hayden. "Save his strength."

"Kaya Sahoro," Lilia whispered. "Quiet, Grandfather," she began to cry softly. "You can tell me later."

But the old man struggled even more. Driven by a force of will, he began to speak, weakly, but clearly, draining him of life. "Shongorabi Nyah-Gwaheh. Walta orapi pokan. Kayendara Windago Kaikut, Tonowa tan shohonto." Reaching into his shirt with bloodied fingers, Stone Bear withdrew a leather pouch. With trembling hands he opened the pouch, revealing its contents of leaves and talismans. Extending the pouch toward Lilia, he nodded his head for her to take it. With tear-filled eyes she looked at him and took the bundle. A faint smile passed across the lips of the Hawate. "Mappo cuska, Nyah-Gwaheh," he whispered faintly, and died in their arms.

Matt watched, wide-eyed as the old man's body slumped lifelessly before his eyes. Almost immediately, the wind from the mesa began to howl down the canyon. At the same instant, from behind them, a low growl seemed to emanate from the cave. "Let's work our way over to the village," Matt shouted above the wind. "That's where I left the horse."

Lifting the Hawate's broken body into his arms, Hayden stood and began to walk haltingly over the crags of the uneven mountain-side. Lilia took out a small flashlight and, cupping her hand over the reflector, carefully lighted their way across the rocks to the cliff dwellings perched on the side of the canyon, one hundred feet away. Each step was awkward and filled with peril as their feet stumbled over the irregular, jagged terrain. At length the worn marks of a path appeared and they found themselves before the towering remains of the Tonowa village—carved out of the canyon wall and crafted with ancient hands. Seeking shelter from the sudden winds, they wove their way into the maze of rock and adobe shelters. Hayden shoved his way past a door banging open and shut in the gusts and laid Stone Bear on an empty cot just inside the entrance. Lilia knelt by the old man's side and reverently took his hand.

Matt secured the door shut and said nothing as the blast of the air outside continued to howl. At length he interrupted her silent mourning. "Lilia," he said, "those Indian words—his last words—what did they mean?"

Lilia remained kneeling on the floor, motionless, focused entirely on the old man. Finally she responded. "They were the words of an ancient tribal prayer—about the hour of Tonowa destiny—and the vengeance of God."

Matt picked up the pouch, which lay on the ground beside Stone Bear. "And this?"

Lilia took the pouch gently from his hand. "It is a totem of sacred emblems. Part of a ritual to ceremonially summon the spirits and to call the Nyah-Gwaheh."

Outside, gusts of wind howled through the village with a swelling fury while the earth seemed to tremble beneath them. And then, mingled with the wail of the rising storm, an unmistakable rumble of a living thing erupted from the bowels of the mountain itself—fierce and angry.

The low growl brought Matt to his natural instincts. He suddenly felt exposed and vulnerable. His rifle was still in the saddle holster with his horse. Without it there was nothing but these walls of adobe to protect them from the elements or the wild. Leaving Lilia momentarily, he slipped out the door and hurried by a narrow trail to a small open area carved into the mountainside. There, growing skittish amidst the whining blasts of wind, stood Thatcher's bay mare. Slowing his pace, Matt carefully approached the horse and reached for his rifle. But as he did so a roar of anger belched forth from the nearby cave and the heart of the mountain. Reacting with instant terror, the horse reared up on two legs and vaulted from the clearing.

Matt tumbled to the ground as the frightened animal bolted down the winding path that wove to the floor of the canyon. He sat up, looked warily around and scrambled to the edge of the clearing. Straining his eyes, he peered through the dark expanse to the wall of the mountain across from the village.

There at the cave entrance, illuminated dimly by the light of the crescent moon, he watched as something huge crawled slowly from the blackness of the cavern. The shapeless mass crouched on the ledge, still as night. Matt squinted to see more when suddenly a pair of eyes reflected the moonlight for the flash of an instant before they disappeared. Something had looked directly at him. And then, the hulking figure began to move in his direction.

Backing away from the edge of the clearing, Matt turned and broke into a run, the wind blowing into his face. He burst into the dwelling where Lilia still knelt beside her grandfather. His entrance startled her, but another roar from the creature on the mountainside brought her to her feet. She looked at Hayden in the dimming beam of the flashlight. The growl came again, closer, and he strained to listen to it.

"Matt," she asked, "what is it?"

Hayden continued to listen, slowly shaking his head. "I don't know." Turning, he closed the open door and barricaded it with an old broken chair that had been left behind. As he finished his vain defense, they heard another snarl, this time very close. Something was lumbering about the perimeter of their hiding place. Whatever it was, it was searching for them. Whatever it was, it had found them.

Helplessly, they looked at one another and began to hear additional noises—sniffing, together with more pronounced growls, and then, the distinct sound of something clawing, scratching, and digging away at the other side of the wall of sun-dried mud. Warily, Hayden approached the interior wall and placed his hand and ear against the rough adobe. Taking a step back, Hayden dropped his hand and stared at the adobe in horror as he backed to the opposite wall. Lilia on the other hand, remained in the center of the room as if staked to the spot. She stood, unafraid, watching the wall where the clawing sounds were heard.

"Lilia," Matt spoke in a low voice. However, the girl did not respond. Reaching out, he took her gently by the hand and backed with her into the far corner of the small room. They both stared at the far wall as the scratching and loud growling continued. Then gradually, a small hole appeared in the adobe until a set of claws began to protrude through the inside of the wall, tearing away small, then larger chunks of the barrier between them and a certain doom. Matt looked around. Snatching up the old chair that had barricaded the door he held it over his shoulder, determined to defend them both.

In that instant, a massive paw smashed through the adobe, creating a jagged, gaping hole in the wall amidst a small cloud of powdered dirt. Matt and Lilia held their breath as the dust settled around a massive hairless paw—momentarily still, suspended in the shadowed yellow light of their flashlight beams. They watched, wide-eyed as long claws extended, lengthening from each digit—four, eight, twelve inches—each a razor-sharp instrument of death. The claws flexed behind muscular toes, reaching further into the room in search of prey. And then, just as suddenly as it had burst through the wall, the paw froze in place again as the claws retracted, and the foot itself pulled back through the jagged hole and disappeared. Matt and Lilia huddled in the corner, listening as the predator retreated, but nothing more followed than an eerie quiet. Only the wailing of the wind remained.

"He's gone," said Lilia.

"But why?" wondered Hayden. He jumped quickly to his feet, and then more carefully approached the opening to look through it. As he did so, Lilia stood, walked curiously to the door, and turned the latch.

"No!" shouted Matt as the door flew open. He leaped across the room and grabbed Lilia, tumbling with her to the ground. They both looked up to see the door, banging against the wall before another series of windy gusts.

"The wind," Matt thought aloud. Getting up he walked to the door and stepped outside. He looked back to Lilia. "The wind shifted. Whatever it was, it lost our scent, or picked up something else."

From across the room Hayden looked at Lilia, still on the floor. Then she began to laugh—a laughter that grew louder and more hysterical. "The wind!" she said, almost to herself. "That's it! It was all the wind. That's all that was out there. Just the wind."

Hayden rushed to her and, kneeling beside her, reached out to touch her arm. "Lilia, it's okay." At his touch she jerked away. He pulled back slightly, but continued to reassure her. "Lilia. It's all over. We're safe for the moment, from whatever it is."

"Safe?" Lilia shouted. "If the Nyah-Gwaheh is real, nobody's safe. Don't you understand that?"

"Yes, I do, Lilia," answered Matt defensively, his voice filling the room. "I saw it too."

"Good," she continued to scream at him. "Then tell me, are you scared?"

Matt grabbed her by the shoulders. "I'm terrified," he shouted back. Strangely, his outburst seemed to quiet her down. Embracing him, she buried her head in his shoulder and cried silently. Slowly, he took her in his arms and held her. For a long moment the only sound was her subdued sobbing. And then she lifted her head.

"Matt, I'm sorry," she whispered, wiping her own tears.

Matt stroked her back comfortingly. "Shh," he soothed. "It's all right. We've all got something to be afraid of now." His eyes wandered across the room and settled on the peaceful figure of Stone Bear out-stretched on the cot. His vision narrowed and he lifted his head. "But your grandfather—he wasn't afraid. He knew exactly what it was, and yet he wasn't afraid. Why?"

Lilia released her embrace and slowly turned to look at Stone Bear. She walked across the shabby room of adobe and dust—and knelt again beside him. Matt followed and laid his hand on her shoulder as she reverently studied the old man. There were no more tears or sighs of mourning. Matt watched her face as a peaceful smile stole across her lips. Then she stood. Tranquility had somehow taken the place of grief. "I'm not afraid anymore," she said without taking her eyes off the Hawate.

Matt gently brought her back to reality. "Lilia, we've got to get out of here." Taking her by the hand, he stood and gently lifted the girl to her feet. "Come on," he said and began to lead her from the dwelling. Suddenly she stopped and, returning to her grandfather, snatched the pouch he had given to her from where it lay on the ground. Smiling down at him one last time, she quietly placed the pouch inside her shirt and hurried off with Hayden.

Chapter 7

NIGHT OF THE NYAH-GWAHEH

The campfire on the canyon floor whipped violently in the gusting wind. Ford and Maddox huddled near it to keep warm. Hicks paced on the opposite side of the fire, animated well beyond his drunkenness.

"It wasn't my imagination, it wasn't the wind, and it wasn't any coyote or mountain lion. There was something up there."

Ford stood impatiently, shaking his fist at Hicks. "You're crazy. And you're drunk."

"Tell me you didn't hear it," shouted Hicks. "You swear to me," he ranted, pointing at Maddox, "that you didn't see something up there, moving around." He gestured wildly to the canyon wall.

Maddox sat in the silence. He stared into the fire as the violence of the wind carried its heat into the night. "I saw it," he said soberly. "I saw—something."

"Stupid childish idiots!!" shouted Ford. "What you saw was shadows in the moonlight and the campfire. The only thing up there was an old Indian. And we dealt with him."

"And what about those growls and snarls, Ford?" asked Maddox, still sitting morosely glaring at the flames. "Those weren't no shadows."

"Then why don't you both go up there and find out what it was?" raved Ford.

"That's what I'm gonna do," shouted Hicks as he picked up his rifle from a pile of gear. He shook the firearm in the air. "I'll go up there and do something about it while you two little girls sit

70

around the campfire in your petticoats keeping your hands warm." He cocked his rifle. "I'm gonna find whatever it is and bring it back to stuff for my trophy room."

Suddenly, the snapping of twigs like the crushing of a tumbleweed resounded in the still darkness behind him. Hicks spun awkwardly, with his rifle poised, and rocked on his heels as he peered into the empty night beyond the light of the fire. All was quiet for several seconds as Hicks slowly smiled, relaxed his grip on the rifle, and lowered it to his side. He took a deep breath and continued to lock his gaze into the night. "I'll bring it down," he slurred with a drunken confidence, "whatever it is."

In that instant, the form of a huge creature rose up from the shadows before him. Standing on its hind legs to a height of over twenty feet, the monster bore the muscular features of a huge bear, covered with a thick grayish-brown hide, overlapping in massive, rhinoceros-like folds all over its body. Towering over the guards in the firelight, the creature gaped open its powerful jaws and tore through a lull in the wind with a ferocious roar.

Hicks screamed as he jerked up his rifle to fire. But before the gun was chest high the beast swung a huge clawed paw at the guard, back-handing him into the campfire like a stuffed toy. Ford and Maddox bolted away in terror as Hicks struggled to his feet, shrieking and in flames. Falling on all fours, the Nyah-Gwaheh reached out and clutched the blazing guard in its claws and cut short his agonizing cries, biting him in half.

From the darkness beyond the campfire, Maddox stopped, took aim with his six-shooter, and fired several times. The creature glanced up, seeming to feel the bullets as mere pin pricks, and charged in the guard's direction. Maddox turned, fleeing in terror.

Meanwhile, Ford had run in the opposite direction, finding momentary protection behind a clump of sagebrush. Seeing the beast break from the campfire after Maddox, he scrambled from the ground and sprinted to their nearby truck. Crawling into the driver's seat, Ford fumbled for the key before he found it and shoved it into the ignition. The truck cranked over with difficulty.

By this time Maddox had emptied his revolver at the monster. The clicks of the useless weapon registered in renewed panic on the face of the drunken guard. Suddenly aware of the churning truck engine barely twenty-five feet away, Maddox dropped his gun and ran exhaustedly in the direction of the laboring vehicle, where Ford still squirmed behind the wheel, struggling with the starter. Maddox was almost there when the ignition finally kicked in. Ford turned to look back in frenzied terror as he jammed the truck into gear and gunned the engine. "Ford," Maddox screamed as he reached to grab onto the vehicle. But the foreman wasn't waiting an instant. Maddox stumbled and fell to the ground. He slowly stood on his feet and staggered to face the beast. The Nyah-Gwaheh stood enraged before him, backlit by the campfire, and roared ferociously as it opened its huge jaws.

Hayden and Lilia had just come over the brow of a rise on the canyon floor. A thunderous roar followed by a scream in the night mingled with the blustering of the wind. Perhaps five hundred feet away, and lighted by a small campfire, they saw a bear-like monster, standing to a full height of a telephone pole, towering over the tiny figure of a crouching man. It rent the air with another roar and then fell full force on its victim. Lilia turned away with a subdued cry, burying her face in Hayden's shoulder. Paralyzed in horror, Matt watched this display of nature in its cruelest, and at the same time, most unbelievable form. The legend of the Nyah-Gwaheh was suddenly terrifyingly real.

In the distance the beast lifted its head and looked around as if it perceived the presence of spectators. Hayden doubled down to his knees, pulling Lilia with him. With eyes accustomed to the darkness, the monster held its gaze in their direction and held perfectly still while a low growl rumbled in its throat. Then, without warning, it belched forth another terrific roar and bounded away toward the exit at the mouth of the canyon.

As Matt and Lilia finally stood again, a thousand different thoughts filled each of their minds. Then another more welcome and familiar sound caught their ears. It was the neighing of a horse. Hayden looked around. Only a hundred feet away he spotted Thatcher's bay mare, its reins snagged amongst the rocks by the mountainside. "We've got no time to lose, Lilia," he said. "That thing is headed in the direction of Thatcher's place."

As he walked away, she quickly caught up with him. "But why the ranch?"

"There's fresh game there," Matt answered, "and he's still hungry."

The two of them approached the frightened horse, which struggled wildly to get away as they came into view. Hayden held up his hands and slowed his advance on the skittish animal. "Okay," Matt calmed her and drew near, finally putting his hand on the mare's shoulder and gently moving it to her neck. "That's it. He's gone," Matt soothed the horse. "But now I need you to take me in his direction again."

Freeing the reins, Hayden quickly climbed on and pulled Lilia up behind him. "What is the quickest way back?" he asked.

"Cut across the canyon to the southeast," answered Lilia. "I'll show you the way. We'll beat it there by five minutes—maybe."

Urging the horse forward, the two rode off at a full gallop to warn the others.

Thatcher, Schindler, and Buck waited anxiously in the great room of the ranch house. The professor had just paced the full length of the room when he stopped and listened. Outside the distant sound of horses' hooves echoed through the night—and grew quickly closer. Glancing at the others he turned and hurried to the door when suddenly Matt and Lilia burst through the entry, breathless.

Thatcher was on his feet. "Matt, Lilia!"

"We've been worried sick," said Schindler.

"Quick Professor, there's no time," Hayden cut him off. He still held his own rifle. "We've seen your bear."

The bearded face of the professor lighted up like a child's on Christmas morning. "What?"

Buck held his enthusiasm in reserve. "Matt, what are you talking about?"

"The Nyah-Gwaheh," broke in Lilia. "It's alive!"

"And well," added Matt.

Schindler, however, was animated beyond restraint. Striding to the coat rack he grabbed his jacket and hat. "I've got to get to the canyon and have a look at it."

Hayden hurried to stand between the professor and the door. "You don't have to go that far."

At that moment a huge claw crashed through the front window of the ranch house. Everyone in the room scattered as the beast grasped wildly at them. The full length of his muscular foreleg reached several feet into the room, casting chairs and end tables into the air as though they were dollhouse toys. Every few seconds the fierce eyes and the razor sharp teeth of the creature would appear at the window as he snarled with anger at his elusive prey. Only the size of the heavy window frame kept the beast from smashing his way into the room to satisfy his hunger and rage.

Everyone instantly took cover or otherwise distanced themselves from the huge armored bear—except Professor Schindler, who stood transfixed, watching the sweeping claw and the face of the creature as it peered in at them. Buck ran back and pulled him to safety, just ahead of the grasping paw.

Hayden, in the meantime, scrambled to a gun rack. Taking the rifles from their pegs, he tossed them to Thatcher, Buck, and finally to Lilia. Matt raised his own Winchester as the others lost no time in taking aim to fire. But barely had they cocked their weapons than Schindler shouted into the din. "Don't shoot unless absolutely necessary."

There was a moment of silence amidst chaos as they all looked at Schindler and each other in mild disbelief—while the creature continued to claw violently at them. After a pause that lasted for a heartbeat, three rifles in the room burst into a blaze of gunfire. Lilia, perched behind a sofa, took careful aim and squeezed on the trigger, only to ease it back as she continued to watch the furious beast through the sight. Slowly and thoughtfully, she lay the rifle down, completely detached from the violence around her. Meanwhile, the others were quickly emptying their guns of their ammunition. But the bullets seemed to take little effect against the monster's armor-like skin.

At the same time the beast had been crashing his massive upper body into the window frame, which was beginning to give way to his strength. Squeezing his head through the crumbling hole, he thrust his foreleg deep into the room.

Matt glanced at his Winchester, then back at the enraged beast, realizing how inadequate it was for the challenge at hand. Pausing to look around the room, he stopped when his eyes settled on a double-barreled shotgun hanging on a rack—beside the window where the beast was advancing. "Mike," he shouted, pointing to the wall. "Is that shotgun loaded?"

"Yeah," bellowed Thatcher. "Guess I mounted it on the wrong wall."

Matt stood from his protection behind a chair. "Just cover me while I get to it. I'm going to try to get outside behind him."

Then, taking a deep breath he shouted, "Now!" Sprinting across the room, Matt sidestepped broken furniture like a linebacker as he raced toward the opposite wall—and the beast. He barely evaded the sweeping paw of the angry creature as he lunged to the gun rack beside the window. Everyone with a rifle, even Lilia, fired their weapons in an effort to distract the creature. But the shooting seemed to enrage him all the more as he forced the other forepaw through the opening. Reaching into the room, the monster grasped at Matt, just as the hunter grabbed the shotgun from the rack. Rolling against the wall, Matt ducked to avoid being impaled by the razor claws and then dove, crashing through the corner window, just ahead of another swipe of the monster's massive foreleg.

The hunter tumbled onto the verandah and stood, dazed as he regained his bearings. Clutching the shotgun, he scrambled beyond the porch and turned to take careful aim at the animal. With a resounding blast he unloaded both barrels at the creature's side.

Unlike the mere annoyance of the other bullets, this shot immediately commanded the full attention of the Nyah-Gwaheh. With a startled jerk, the beast wrenched himself from the wreck of the ranch house, showering the ground with broken remnants of the porch railing and shattered window. Rearing back, he faced Matt.

As he did so, large chunks of debris rained over the hunter, knocking him off his feet. He struck the ground with a jolt, jarring the shotgun from his grasp and sending it disappearing into the darkness. He quickly rolled over to look for it when an ear-splitting roar from the beast convinced him to abandon his search. Staggering to his feet, he dashed away, with the Nyah-Gwaheh in close pursuit.

Sprinting around the corner of the ranch house, Matt turned to glance behind him when another ferocious roar in front of him froze him in his tracks. Jerking his head forward in terror, he found himself face to face with a mountain lion, snarling angrily behind the grate of his cage. The other animals of the professor's menagerie began to howl and roar in suit.

Hayden breathed a sigh, but his relief was only momentary. Instantly, the furious roar of the Nyah-Gwaheh split the night air behind him. Spinning around, he ducked instinctively and dove to the ground as the monster took an angry swing at him—and missed, tearing into the cougar cage. Without a pause, the irate cat lashed viciously at the huge creature's threatening claw. Startled, the Nyah-Gwaheh drew back the scratched paw and hesitated, examining it. As he did so, Matt inched away from the distracted creature.

For the moment, the beast was totally unaware of the hunter. Scrutinizing his wounds, the beast flexed the toes of its paw and looked at the snarling creatures in the cages with a blend of determination and mild curiosity. Reaching out, the Nyah-Gwaheh began to tear open the thick wire wall of the cougar cage while the growling cats inside crouched away from the claws, which were ripping a hole into their enclosure. Suddenly and without warning, the four freed animals leaped through the opening, attacking the beast at once.

By this time, the others arrived from the ranch house to the edge of the cage yard. Several of Thatcher's ranch hands had also joined them. They raised their guns to shoot.

"No, don't!" Hayden shouted. They held their fire. "Believe me, it's not the best way to make friends. Besides, he's distracted for the moment."

"He's right," agreed Schindler. "Let's see if nature can take care of this on its own."

Thatcher was more practical. "I'd suggest we take cover," he warned, "or nature's likely to take care of us. These animals are angry." Responding to the boss, the ranchers began to back away and make room for the lethal combat.

Indeed, in the courtyard, nature was taking its course. Attacking together, the several cougars clawed at the hide of the Nyah-Gwaheh as he furiously swiped and tore at them. Their only advantage was numbers as he twisted and writhed to grab them or shake them away. But ultimately, they were no match for the creature. One by one he sunk his claws into the lions, hurling them away with terrifying ferocity.

At last, two of the mountain lions remained—one taunting him on the ground and another clinging to his back. Thrashing to reach the animal on his back, the monster toppled onto a stack of cages holding a dozen desert coyotes. Freed from their captivity, these too joined the cougars in their attack of the Nyah-Gwaheh. However, the creature was quick to adapt to the onslaught of the smaller predators and he rolled to crush them on the ground or snatched them as they leaped toward him. Finally, one remaining mountain lion sprang at his head. Struggling to tear the vicious cat from his face, the monster stumbled backward, crashing through the bars of a large enclosure. There on his back, he dragged the clawing creature down his face to his jaws. With a vengeance he opened his mouth and crushed the cat between two rows of razor-sharp fangs before casting it aside.

Rolling from his back, the Nyah-Gwaheh stood upright in the ruins of the broken cage and roared ferociously. Suddenly the roar was cut short. The creature toppled to the ground, attacked from behind. The huge grizzly bear, whose cage had just been destroyed, fell angrily on top of the thick-skinned monster and then stood to his full height to pounce on his opponent again. Standing almost twelve feet tall, the ferocious furred beast raised its claws and sunk them with all of his weight into the intruder.

Roaring in pain, the Nyah-Gwaheh folded its hind legs and kicked the grizzly across the remains of the splintered cage. Rolling to it side, the armored bear began to struggle to its feet when the grizzly attacked again. The two of them tumbled from the enclosure into the clearing of the cage yard. Ranch hands, watching the spectacle, scattered to avoid being crushed amidst this contest of savagery— arbitrated by the most primitive law of the jungle.

The two animals shook loose of each other and struggled upright to fight again. At over twenty feet, the Nyah-Gwaheh towered above the grizzly. But the fur-covered bear hardly seemed to acknowledge the size of his opponent. Without a pause, the smaller beast charged forward, knocking the invader to its side and sinking his teeth into the monster's armored shoulder. It rose for another attack when the Nyah-Gwaheh lashed out with a muscular foreleg, sending his foe sprawling to the ground. Springing awkwardly to its feet, the larger animal fell instantly on the grizzly, digging his talons deep into the smaller beast's ribs. Bawling in rage, the grizzly twisted from the Nyah-Gwaheh and returned the attack. But another swing of the monster's foreleg sent the smaller bear collapsing to the ground again. Then, with a vicious snarl, the Nyah-Gwaheh fell on him with all of its weight, its razor claws sinking deep and its powerful jaws ripping violently into the grizzly's throat. A final agonizing roar pierced the night and the beast fell silent as the Nyah-Gwaheh devoured the blood and meat of its defeated cousin.

From any protective cover they could find, the spectators of the contest watched only momentarily in horrified amazement before the beast rose again to its full height and rent the air with an ear-shattering roar. Having vanquished all foes, the monster glanced almost dismissively at the tiny humans in the remains of the cage yard and then slowly turned and retreated in the direction of the canyon and its cave.

The ranchers stood transfixed until the creature disappeared from sight. Schindler was the first to speak. "Magnificent!" he said in hushed tone. It was almost reverent. "I must see it again."

Hayden stepped out in front of him, if only to have his full attention. "If that thing doesn't get fed again tomorrow, I think you can count on it."

"By all means, we're going to feed it," Schindler said enthusiastically as he looked around at the others. "Anything to get close enough to study it. Why, we've got the paleontological find of the century here."

"Oh no you don't," came a voice from behind them. They all turned to look.

Jeremy Webb stood at the edge of the ranch house. Beside him stood Ford, Simmons, and several other miners. More reinforcements were arriving in trucks behind them.

Webb continued. "You haven't got anything. And neither you, nor anybody else is going to feed or study that monster. Because by this time tomorrow, it's going to be dead."

"We're going to make sure of it," chimed in Ford, hefting a rifle.

"You can't be serious," Professor Schindler approached Webb in amazement. "That creature is a prehistoric miracle. Its discovery could rewrite the science of the earth's past. You can't destroy an animal of such value."

"Who says we can't!" growled Ford. "That thing murdered two of my buddies up there tonight."

"Is that so?" challenged Hayden. He leered at Ford knowingly.

Schindler was oblivious to the exchange. "Webb," he appealed, "you're not so much a butcher that you could throw away such a find. Let us go in that cave and capture the creature. Give us the opportunity at least."

"Sorry, Professor," said Webb coldly. "Simmons."

Clark Simmons, stepped forward with self-importance. "By order of the Interior Department," he said officiously, "I am hereby declaring martial law on the Tonowa Reservation. Until that creature is killed, no one will be permitted in the canyon, and to enter the cave will be considered trespassing, under the severest penalty of the law."

Chapter 8

GAMES IN THE DARKNESS

By the light of dawn the floor of the Canyon de Dios was already alive with activity. Dozens of miners, weapons in hand, stood vigil at the base of the towering cliffs to enforce martial law. At the other end of the valley small trucks continued to bring in mining materials and heavy equipment, all guarded by watchful employees of Mammoth Steel.

From the heights of the cliffs, the entire panorama resembled a patch of dry sand, swarming with so many ants. Lilia peered down at the valley floor between two rocks just below the rim of Oscura Mesa. Behind her the rest of the party lowered themselves onto a level stretch of ground tucked into the side of the mountain. Tom and a few other braves were helping Schindler, Buck, Thatcher, and several ranch hands onto the clearing. The girl turned to look at them and signaled silently for them to stay low to the ground. Hayden was the last to descend to the spot. Handing his rifle to Tom, he lowered himself onto the flat. They all crouched low against the canyon wall under the cover of predawn light.

"Thanks," he said, taking his gun from the Indian. "You're sure we can't be seen up here from the floor of the canyon?"

Tom smiled. "I grew up in this desert, Hayden. And this canyon was my playground. I know every crevice on the face of the rock wall. They couldn't spot us if they were looking for us."

Buck, overhearing, voiced a reasonable concern. "Yeah, but how close will they be guarding the mouth of that cave?"

"After last night," chipped in Thatcher, "how close would you be?"

The members of the party all laughed—though nervously. Lilia joined them and spoke quietly. "That's about the size of it. There's a lot of movement down there, but so far, they're keeping their distance from the canyon wall. My guess is they'll wait until he's hungry again, later in the day, before they try to lure him out."

Schindler finally spoke. "Well as they say, 'the coast is clear.' Tom," he turned to the brave and nodded, "lead the way."

Carefully, the group moved forward, keeping as close as possible to the wall of the canyon and out of the line of sight from the ground. Tom led them in a twisting trail of bends, switchbacks, and sudden descents, along a pathway that none could have seen without him or the two other braves who served as their guides. More than once they had to crawl on all fours to ensure they had the cover of the mountainside to protect them. But then suddenly they came to a drop of fifteen feet, hidden from the valley floor by a huge crag of natural stone. Tom descended first to demonstrate the footings and handholds carved into the wall. Every member of the party carefully followed until they all stood again on level ground.

"Stay low," said Tom. And rounding the crag, the group found themselves standing before the sacrificial altar and huge mouth of the cave.

Schindler was amazed and pleased. "Nice work, Tom."

"Yeah," acknowledged the brave, "but this is as far as I can guide you." He pointed to the cave. "I've never been in there, but I'm ready to go." Then he looked at Matt. "So, what's the next move, Hayden?"

Matt was ready. He knew the next part of this expedition was under his leadership. "Okay. We're a lot better armed than we were last night. Everybody's got a .375 H&H Mag caliber rifle that should be able to penetrate that armor skin of his. Some of you have revolvers for good measure. Of course, we know that smaller caliber bullets don't hurt him. But he doesn't seem to like them much either. So let's hope we can at least defend ourselves."

"But," spoke up Schindler, "killing it is a last resort."

"Yes," Tom raised his voice. "Did everyone hear the professor? It must not be killed!" he said emphatically. "The Nyah-Gwaheh belongs to the Tonowa."

"He might disagree," muttered Buck. "That beast doesn't think he belongs to anybody." The Tonowa braves began to murmur.

Matt broke in, anxious to quell any controversy before it began. "Ownership isn't the point. Our goal is to capture the Nyah-Gwaheh before Webb and his men have a chance to destroy it. Because if that happens, it won't matter who he belongs to. Let's just do what we came for—get in there and draw him into the open. Once he's out of the cave, I can nail him with this." Lifting his leather case, he unzipped it and pulled out a unique looking rifle, with a ¾-inch barrel that extended back along the stock. It was a contrast to his traditional Winchester.

He held the weapon up. "This is a prototype for what is called a tranquilizer gun. I've got enough sedative in this thing to put King Kong to sleep, if I can get a clear shot at him. But it's no good to us inside the cave. Like I said, we've got to get him outdoors," he leaned the gun on the sacrificial altar, "where I can use it. Understood?"

The men all nodded their heads as they studied the gun.

"Lilia," Matt spoke directly to her, "you keep an eye on this for me." She doffed her own hat in silent acknowledgment. "Meanwhile," he raised his voice again, "Lilia is going to stand guard out here and signal us if anyone is on their way into the cave."

"What if we're too deep into the cave to hear any signal?" asked Hank, the ranch foreman.

The men all looked to Matt anxiously. "Then, gentlemen, we'll be on our own. Honestly, we have no idea how deep we're going. From the moment we go into that cave, we'll be in uncharted territory." He stopped and looked around. "Anybody want to reconsider?"

He waited for a long moment, staring at the ground. No one spoke or stirred.

Buck came up to Matt and handed him his familiar Winchester. "Thanks," he nodded and turned to enter the cave. But on the brink of the entrance he stopped and turned, looking around slowly at everyone on the ledge. "My friends," he said soberly, "a good man,

Stone Bear, gave his life on this ground last night, sacrificed as literally as any animal that was ever laid on that altar. I stood at the mouth of this cave with him just yesterday, qualifying to know and see things he considered sacred." Matt paused and swallowed hard. "This place meant something to him. This creature meant something to him. As each of us crosses this threshold, I hope we'll consider what it all means to us."

Matt paused. "Well," he took one more look around at the solemn ranchers and Indians, but with nothing more to really say, he shrugged and sighed. He stole one last glance at Lilia, who smiled with quiet gratitude. He nodded again and entered the cave, followed by the others.

Crossing the threshold, the ten explorers were enveloped in a deepening gloom. Like the clutching fingers of a great fist, the shadows quickly closed around them, drawing them into the darkness. Within seconds the hunting party found themselves completely shut off from the light of day. Flashlights flicked on as they pushed ahead in a tense silence. Freakish lights and shadows reflected off the walls of the cavern, vaguely illuminating the tense determination of the men as they trudged carefully down the tunnel. They gradually descended while the cavern widened. Then, one by one, each man stopped as the beams of their lights shown on the wall of the cave. Transfixed before the ancient snapshot of the attacking Nyah-Gwaheh, they all stared in awe at the myth that they now knew was reality—a reality waiting for them in the depths of the cave. Etched into the volcanic rock and painted in colors undimmed by the centuries, the tableau of terror provided a warning that was clear without translation. This was the barrier beyond which man was forbidden to tread.

Matt swallowed. "If anybody's afraid of monsters," he said soberly, "Now's the time to turn back. No hard feelings." Each man looked around at his comrades and then back to Hayden. "All right then."

Taking the lead again, Matt walked past the "warning sign" followed by the others.

Buck turned to Thatcher, walking beside him in the darkness. "I thought you didn't do caves?" he asked.

"Yeah," Thatcher answered with a bitter single laugh. "Lousy time to try something new."

But, by and large, there was little conversation in the darkness. The men marched forward in uncomfortable silence. Each man's head was filled with his own thoughts, his own worries, and his own misgivings. They walked for about five minutes, which seemed more like an hour when, from somewhere seemingly far in the distance, a low growl echoed through the cave. It was instantly answered with the cocking of half a dozen rifles in the shadows as the men came to a halt.

"Keep your heads, boys," cautioned Thatcher. "And save your ammunition. That rumble was still a long way off."

Suddenly the men heard the noise of falling rocks in the cave.

Buck voiced what every man was thinking. "That sounded a little closer."

"How far?" asked Thatcher.

Tom Running Wolf squinted into the darkness, considering. "A couple of hundred feet?" he glanced at Hayden for confirmation.

"Three hundred at most," answered Matt.

Led by Hayden, the group continued down the cave, the silence of the cavern only broken by their echoing footsteps. Within a few feet the cave opened up into a still larger chamber. Without a word, Matt paused and gestured to the left as the direction to follow. Schindler and the others behind him nodded in assent and then continued forward. But as they proceeded they were startled by another tumble of rocks to their right, this time much closer. Everyone reacted instantly, some throwing themselves against the far wall of the cave, while a few others crouched to one knee with their rifles drawn.

Frozen in place they waited in the silence as Thatcher swung his flashlight in the direction of the sound. The beam of the light revealed nothing but another tunnel. Straightening he gestured with his flashlight. "I was sure that last sound came from this direction."

"It did," said Hayden without emotion.

"It was also further down than this," concurred Schindler.

"I don't like this, boss," said Hank.

"Me neither," agreed one of the ranch hands. Others murmured in assent.

The Indian braves were also listening and glancing at one another. "Tom," said one of them. "These have been warnings. We are in grave danger here."

As the words were leaving his lips, Buck, standing at the rear of the group, noticed a trickle of dust falling from the ceiling. "Matt!" he screamed as a growl pierced the air behind them.

Instantly several flashlight beams twisted into the air illuminating the face of the Nyah-Gwaheh in a connecting cave overhead. Without hesitation several men swung their guns to fire. "No!" shouted Tom as the flash of gunshots ignited the darkness and blasts reverberated through the air. At the same time the growl of the Nyah-Gwaheh erupted into a roar as rocks began to fall in a landslide from the ceiling. The terrific sound of the crashing stones blended with the screams of the men as lights flashed throughout the cave. Everyone scrambled in a mad dash for life amidst the collapse of the cave roof.

For a moment, the cavern seemed to be collapsing around them. Then as suddenly as it began, the thunderous terror of the cave-in stopped—its roar replaced by the tumbling of errant rocks and the coughing of the hunters. Flashlight beams showed dimly through the dust that filled the cave. Hayden had taken refuge into a side tunnel with the professor. Schindler was hacking as Matt helped him up. "Are you all right, Professor?"

"Yes," he coughed, looking around. "Where is that creature?"

"Gone, for the present," explained Matt. "Otherwise this would all be over by now."

"Then what about the others?" asked Schindler as he struggled to his feet.

"Mike! Buck!" Matt called.

"We're over here," Thatcher's voice sounded dully from the settling dust.

Half feeling his way and half following his flashlight beam, Hayden staggered through the haze to where his comrades were huddled. "Tom's been hurt," explained Thatcher. "But I think we're all alive."

"Oh, it's not that bad," said Tom, holding his head and struggling to sit up. Blood trickled through his fingers. "I'm okay."

"Yeah." It was Buck's voice from the other side of the cave. "But we're not." Standing from the floor, Hayden, Schindler, and the others joined Buck, who was examining the rockslide with his flashlight. "This isn't good." The beams of their lights shone all around the collapsed tunnel—the same tunnel that led to the exit. The dust was still settling around the cave in, blocking their escape. "We're completely cut off."

"True enough," agreed Thatcher as he shined his light up to where the Nyah-Gwaheh had ambushed them. A tumble of rocks filled the space where the monster had been. "But we're also cut off from him."

"So, you're saying, he can't get to us?" smiled Buck.

Matt, standing nearby, merely shrugged. "Well, not for the moment."

"What are you getting at?" asked Buck.

Hayden looked around the large room in the darkness. "The Nyah-Gwaheh has lived here for hundreds of years. He knows these caves like any of us knows our own house or like Tom knows the walls of the canyon. Meanwhile, inside this mountain we are lost, literally groping in the darkness without a roadmap—completely at his mercy in his environment."

"And yet," pondered Schindler, "he doesn't attack."

"Exactly," said Hayden. "Instead he seems to be toying with us—playing a morbid game of hide and seek. And it's a good game too. Your beast is hiding just well enough to lure us in circles without getting caught. He's intelligent."

"But why the game?" asked Thatcher.

Schindler's face suddenly brightened and he looked at Hayden, who was also grinning as he looked at him. They had both reached the same conclusion. "How incredibly simple," he said smiling.

Hayden voiced their united thought. "He isn't hungry."

"But what happens when he gets hungry?" asked Buck.

At that moment, Tom's voice called from a corner of the cavern. "Hey, come look at this!" Joining Tom, the group followed the downward beam of his flashlight. There at their feet, a large hole gaped through the floor. Dust and dirt were still falling from its edges. "This is where the boulder fell that almost killed me. It smashed a hole into another tunnel."

Hayden crouched to study the opening, and then smiled as he glanced up at Schindler. "Gentlemen," he said, looking around at the others, "this is just what we needed. The Nyah-Gwaheh has provided us with a trail that isn't on his map."

Chapter 9

GATEWAY TO THE UNDERWORLD

One at a time, the hunters noiselessly slipped through the hole in the cavern to the level beneath it. Their single-file descent was facilitated by a stair-like formation in the rock, which jutted downward almost twenty feet to the floor level of the connecting tunnel. Once they had all gathered at the bottom, Hayden gestured them silently forward.

"How far do you think . . . ," whispered Buck.

"Shh," Hayden cut him off as he laid a hand on his shoulder. "Not now," he mouthed and held his finger to his lips, before turning to lead them down the new passageway.

Hiking in the semi-darkness, the group marched forward in silence for fifteen minutes. But the silence was the anxious quiet of suspense—not merely for the knowledge that they were attempting to elude a predator on his own turf. Other realities began to feed their uneasiness.

Arriving at a fork in the tunnel, Matt stopped and the others came to a halt behind him.

"Which way?" whispered Hayden.

"Does it matter?" answered Buck in an undertone.

"What does that mean?" shot back Hayden.

"Look at them, Matt," he gestured to the passageways. "They both go downhill. We've been steadily sinking deeper for a quarter of an hour."

"It's not as though we had a choice, Buck," defended Schindler. "This tunnel only goes one direction."

"Yeah," added Thatcher, "down—and as near as I can tell, west. We are going further and further from the cave entrance."

Schindler nodded thoughtfully. "Long, straight, and in one descending direction. That's because it's not an ordinary tunnel," he said. "We've been walking in a volcanic tube."

"A warm volcanic tube," Tom spoke up for the first time in several minutes. "Have you noticed the temperature in here? It's getting hotter as we go lower. I thought this was a dead cave." He looked at Schindler.

The older man nodded. "It's supposed to be. But it seems to grow more alive the deeper we go."

The group fell silent again as they pondered their predicament in the light of these new realities. Thatcher finally spoke. "On the bright side, we haven't heard from our friend for a while," he said. "I think we lost him."

"Well," considered Hayden, slightly annoyed, "I didn't want to lose him completely."

"I'm not so sure you have," corrected Schindler. "Listen."

All the men stopped whispering and listened in the darkness. Far away, down the more steeply inclining of the two tunnels, they heard sounds—not the identifiable growls of the Nyah-Gwaheh, but a myriad unrecognizable noises, muffled by the distance. Matt's eyes narrowed as he strained to hear the weird echoes. Gradually he turned to the professor.

Schindler's expression also begged for an explanation. Hayden slowly shook his head. "It's not like anything I've heard before."

"Well," said the professor, "I say we have a look."

Schindler took one step down the mysterious passage when Matt stopped him. "Wait a minute, Professor. You're determined to go down that tunnel, and I'll go with you." Then he turned to the eight other men. "But none of the rest of you are obligated to come along. This other passageway," he gestured to the alternative tunnel, "appears to be leveling off. Who knows, it may even be the way back to the entrance. Nobody will think less of you if you'd prefer to take it rather than follow us."

He waited. In the beams of their flashlights the ranchers and the Indians looked around at each other. Thatcher fumbled in his pocket for a stick of gum. Buck merely smiled. They both had made their decision already. Then Tom Running Wolf spoke. "Lead the way, Hayden. Whatever's down there may be what we came for. Besides," he grinned, "I'm kinda curious."

"All right," Matt sighed, "and thanks. I don't think either of us wanted to go down there without you. Let's find out what we've got."

Resolutely they all followed Matt and Schindler through the opening and into the tunnel, which twisted at a right angle and then widened into a cave some fifteen feet in diameter before plunging steeply into the heart of the mountain. The previously muffled noises were now noticeably louder as they reverberated off the walls of the cave.

Suddenly Schindler stopped. Hayden and the rest of the group instinctively stopped with him. "What is it, Professor?"

"Everyone," Schindler said, "turn off your flashlights." The men looked at each other, slightly perplexed.

Mike Thatcher was a little more trusting—and compliant. "You heard the professor, boys. Unless you're afraid of the dark." He flipped off his lantern, followed by several others. The effect was breathtaking and awesome. The cave continued to be illuminated by a thousand streams of blue light, embedded into the walls of igneous rock. Hayden held out his hand in front of him, surprised to be able to discern every line and detail, so intense was the florescent glow from the sides, ceiling, and even the floor of the cave.

"There is a concentration of phosphorescence in this volcanic rock that is astounding—literally providing an internal source of light, independent of the sun. It partially explains the existence of the Nyah-Gwaheh—as well as what we may find ahead. Nature has given a new expression of life—here in the depths of the earth."

Unable to contain his own excitement, the professor forged ahead. But his enthusiasm fueled the others with anticipation—just as the natural subterranean light illuminated their way. Any anxiety over the unknown had dissipated in the glow surrounding them, and a childlike sense of adventure led them forward.

And then, suddenly, the broad passageway opened wide before them and they stood together, mesmerized as they gazed in amazement at the spectacle of natural wonder. Standing on an outcropping of volcanic rock they found themselves at the threshold of a vast cavern stretching perhaps a thousand feet from one side to the other and easily one hundred feet high. Waterfalls cascaded from overhead clefts into numerous subterranean pools, reflecting their phosphorescent radiance upon the walls and ceiling of the grotto. Soft greens blending with dim hues of violet and blue clothed the grotto in a diffused radiance of breathtaking, incandescent beauty.

But amidst the subterranean splendor, the cavern was also teeming with life. Scattered across the underground landscape sprang a wide array of vegetation. At once colorless in the dim fluorescence, the undergrowth also seemed to give off a light of its own. And crawling along the grotto floor, or settled in the water of countless pools was the shadow of movement and the miracle of animal life.

For several minutes no one spoke as they each stood in astonished awe—observing this world they had discovered in the midst of the mountain.

Schindler was the first to break the stunned silence. "It's like a pocket in time. Something left over from the Triassic and Jurassic periods over 250 million years ago. All concentrated in an environment that has developed and adapted into an ecosystem unique unto itself." He paused for a long moment. "Gentlemen, what we have here is a veritable wealth of prehistoric knowledge."

Hayden stepped to the edge of the outcropping for a wider look around. "But the real prize doesn't seem to be home."

"No," Schindler confirmed, "we'd know it if he was. This is his world—a realm where he reigns supreme. Here he is a god."

Stepping forward, Buck raised his camera for a photograph of the incredible menagerie. Schindler interrupted him. "Buck, much as I would like a picture of this, I wouldn't advise it. The flash would rouse them. And many of the occupants of this era, even the small ones, were ravenous flesh eaters."

Buck soberly lowered his camera and pointed to a creature about the size of a prize hog at a state fair lumbering by on all fours below them. It had a parrot-like beak and a shield or frill extending back from its forehead. "How about this guy?" he asked.

"That appears to be a small Protoceratops—a plant eater. He's safe."

At that instant a loud squawk pierced the air behind them. Startled, the men turned to look back into the passageway. There, at the opening to the cave stood half a dozen oversized lizards standing upright like large kangaroos. Bobbing their heads in a bird-like fashion, they held their forefeet in front of them, flexing their toes as they studied the party of intruders who were frozen in place.

"How about these, Professor?" asked Buck in an undertone.

"I believe these are Hypsilphodons," he answered. "They're omnivorous."

"Meaning what?" asked Thatcher.

Schindler swallowed. "They can go either way."

Suddenly, one of the lizards sprang toward the group of men. Without hesitation, a rancher in front drew his rifle and fired at the attacking creature. Staggering back, the beast collapsed amidst the others who retreated slightly and joined together in a discordant symphony of horrific shrieks. As quickly as they had done so, they began again to carefully advance and retreat in steps, looking for the opportunity to strike. More of the creatures came to the mouth of the cave behind them.

"Let's go," shouted Matt.

"Where?" yelled Tom.

"Off this shelf. And quickly," he cocked and aimed his rifle. "I'll run interference up here. Go," he shouted. "All of you, get moving."

Scrambling to the edge, the men quickly began to clamber down the outcropping to the floor of the cavern while Hayden and the lead rancher held off the Hypsilphodons. The cowboy fired indiscriminately while Matt was more selective. "Conserve your bullets," he yelled. At that moment the rancher's rifle clicked. Empty. It took the big lizards only a moment to seize the advantage. Leaping en masse, four of the creatures sent him sprawling to the ground as they attacked with their clawed feet poised in the air. As the man screamed, Matt raised his rifle to fire when another of the beasts blindsided him. His rifle clattered over the precipice behind him as he struggled with his attacker, hanging over the edge. With both hands he held the neck of the lizard, while the forearms of the creature swiped violently at him, tearing his shirt. He felt the clawed hind feet of the lizard ripping at his belt in an effort to disembowel him. At that instant a shot rang out and the creature's jaws opened wide in pain as it dropped lifelessly and rolled from him. Matt turned and looked over the edge of the outcropping.

Tom Running Wolf stood at the base of the rock with his rifle still poised upward. "Get down here, Hayden, quickly." Matt glanced at his comrade on the shelf. His screaming had stopped as the huge lizards covered his body. Matt shuddered, tumbled from the shelf, and struggled to the ground where the others were waiting for him. They were all scanning their new surroundings in search of danger.

Hayden staggered to his feet. The others made no effort to leave as they continued to vigilantly look around. Thatcher, holding two rifles, gave Matt back his Winchester. He caught Hayden's eyes and glanced upward toward the outcropping and the cave. "What about Bill?" he asked simply. Averting his eyes to the ground, Matt only shook his head.

Taking a deep breath Hayden stepped to the front of the group. "What is our condition here?"

"We've awoken anther world," said Schindler soberly.

Hayden stopped to listen and strained his eyes to see. As if stirred from a long slumber by the shrieks of the Hypsilphodons and the echo of rifle shots, the cavern was indeed coming to life, slowly erupting with a cacophony of nature's cries. All around them the grotto was beginning to move with prehistoric vitality, until now camouflaged in the water, the foliage, and the blue-green light.

"You're still leading this safari," said Tom. "So which is the way out?"

Matt had been scanning the grotto. "Over there," he finally pointed to a corner of the cavern where a cluster of tunnels provided alternate possible escape routes. "We can go directly through no man's land, or we can work our way around the edge of the grotto. Any preferences?"

"I've got no desire to go through the petting zoo," said Buck. "I vote the long way around." The others all nodded and grunted in assent.

"Stay close together," was the hunter's only command as he forged ahead without looking back. Following Hayden and trying not to draw any attention to themselves, the men edged their way, single file, around the periphery of the grotto. Their pathway led them through thickets of bromeliads, waist-high ferns, and broad-leafed grasses adapted to absorb the dim phosphorescent light of the cavern. Flowers of dull reds, oranges, and purples stood out on the otherwise monochrome hue of the bland vegetation. Palm trees that appeared almost gray and ashen clumps of bamboo sprang here and there, fringing countless pools of rippling water across the open space. The subterranean waterfalls cascading from the walls high overhead created small rivers of life-giving moisture throughout the cave. Collecting in ponds and smaller pools, the water spilled from one level to another and eventually ran off through crevices in the walls of the cave, flowing, perhaps, into another cavern.

"Stay away from the water," shouted Matt. Just then a large group of thin, biped reptiles the size of large chickens leaped from a thicket of ferns, twenty feet up ahead. Stopping curiously when they saw the men, they froze in place. "Stand still," said Hayden. The men stood motionless.

"What do you say, Professor?" asked Thatcher just above a whisper. "Friend or foe."

"Those look like Compsognathus," concluded Schindler. "Compies," he repeated softly. "They are related to birds. Look, they even travel in flocks."

"But do they want to eat us?" clarified Buck in an undertone.

"Oh," said Schindler, snapped back to the real world. "Yes—if they're hungry."

At that instant the "flock" of Compies pierced the air with a chorus of terrifying screeches and dashed headlong at the group of frightened men. The hunters immediately began to fire into the attacking lizards, scattering them in every direction. Still the tiny dinosaurs continued to swarm at them by the dozens, with their jaws snapping wildly. The onslaught of smaller predators momentarily unnerved and overwhelmed the men as they slowly backtracked toward the wall of the cavern.

One of the braves carelessly stepped into the shallows of a large lake. Even amidst the gunfire, the sound of the splash instinctively attracted Hayden's attention. Turning, he shouted. "Get out of the water!"

Tom glanced behind him as well. "Dan!" He reached for the brave. But it was too late. In a lightning quick motion, a set of thin, foot-long jaws sprang from the water, grabbing Dan by the leg. He screamed as he toppled face first into the shoals and then disappeared into the deeper water with only a short gurgling cry. In an instant he was gone. And in that instant, with the attention of the party diverted for a split second, the Compies were upon them in merciless mass attack. Their guns and rifles were suddenly useless against this assault of snapping mouths, razor-like claws, and tiny, needle-sharp teeth. Practically every man fell to the ground, writhing against the onslaught as the Compies swarmed them like piranhas in a feeding frenzy. Then, just as quickly as they had fallen upon the hunters, they broke off the attack, leaped off the men, and slowly, cautiously retreated.

Hayden struggled dizzily from the ground. There were bite marks on his arms and through the torn legs of his blue jeans. The others were likewise scarred from the assault, but alive. Just beyond them the Compies looked around warily as they continued to back away. None of the hunters had a moment to consider the strange behavior of this prehistoric swarm. For no sooner had they righted themselves than a beast bounded into the clearing through a copse of bamboo. Extending almost three yards from his snout to the tip of his tail, the creature resembled a crocodile on two legs—and took no immediate interest in the men. Instead he leaped forward and snatched and swallowed two or three of the chicken-sized lizards whole, before scattering the rest and disappearing in pursuit of them.

Schindler was bleeding from a bite mark on his cheek, but took no notice of it as he sat up, watching the drama of the wild. "Ornithosuchus!" he mused. "Incredible."

Hayden stared at the starry-eyed paleontologist. He had neither the will nor the time to respond. "Get up," he yelled after a split second. The men struggled to stand, groaning and wincing as they staunched the blood from open lacerations. But they had been delivered, for the moment. Matt stood and jerked Buck up from the ground. "Get moving!" he shouted again. "Now may be our only chance. This way."

The men responded almost immediately, following Matt in a desperate hope of escaping the cavern—and surviving with a story to tell their grandchildren. The grotto was no longer the subterranean paradise that had welcomed their eyes only a few minutes before. It was now a bleak world of impending death—a colorless jungle of uncertain doom for each of them. As they quickly vacated the clearing, only the professor lagged irresistibly behind. Taking one second to examine a broad-leafed plant, he reached down and snapped off a piece of foliage the size and shape of a serving platter. Holding it gently, he hurried to catch up with the others.

Staggering through the pale grass at the edge of the cavern, the men looked desperately in all directions as they followed Matt—making their way toward the cluster of caves that were now less than one hundred feet away. Suddenly Hayden came to a dead stop and the group halted behind him. Expressionless, they stared in bleak dismay at the scene before them—a grey expanse of motionless water, reflecting the dull light of the sloping ceiling. Fifty feet across, the forbidding pool barred their way to the gaping fissures that were their only hope of escape.

A silent horror filled Matt's heart—an unspoken anxiety that he knew was overwhelming every man behind him. Scanning the shadowed waters, he couldn't see an inlet or overflow. "Okay," he tried to sound positive. He pointed to the jagged rocks scattered in the dead lake. "This water seems to be shallow and stagnant. There's not much that could hide in there or would want to."

"Shallow or not," reasoned Thatcher, "it's the only way out."

"So, how do we find out how deep it is?" asked Buck.

"Here's one way," answered Tom. Rushing past the other men, Tom splashed into the shallow marsh and ran across the pool. Glancing quickly between his pathway and the other side, he side-stepped rocks and small clumps of hoary grass, which pierced the water's surface. Never did his feet sink more than a half a foot into the shallows as he zigzagged his way to the opposite shore. Turning on the bank, he waved his hands in triumph. "It's shallow enough," he cried, "and it's solid."

"All right," called Matt. "Let's take this single file." Patting the cowboy nearest him on the back, he encouraged him forward. "We're almost there, boys." Suddenly he was interrupted by an ear-splitting shriek in the cavern behind them. With a quick glance, he shoved one of his comrades, then another into the shallow pond. "Go," he shouted, "and don't look back."

Quickly the men dashed, one after another, into the shoals and across the pool. In the midst of the anxious procession, Professor Schindler splashed out to the middle of the water. Stumbling over something soft in the shallows, he lost hold of his precious prehistoric leaf and turned to catch it as it fluttered into the water. "Let it go, Joe," Thatcher called out looking back at Schindler.

But as the professor reached down to retrieve the leaf, a snakelike creature the size of a large python suddenly sprang from the shallow bottom of the silent pond and entwined itself around Schindler's arms and legs. In the span of one second, the professor tumbled into the water, wrapped in a living cable nearly four inches in diameter and over ten feet long.

"Help!" screamed the professor.

From both sides of the pond, men ran to his aid. One of the ranchers raised his rifle to fire. "No," shouted Thatcher, "you'll kill both of them." Falling into the water, he struggled to lift Schindler out of the shallows, while the others fought desperately to free the professor from the pincer grip of the serpent. All the while they dodged the reach of the creature's gaping jaws and powerful, thrashing tail.

Thatcher held Schindler out of the water when the python suddenly turned on him and struck at him with tremendous force.

"Mike!" shouted Buck just in time for Thatcher to grab the snake by the neck with both hands. But both hands were hardly enough to restrain the head and the open jaws only inches from his face. In that instant a resounding blast echoed off the water and through the cave as a rifle shot sliced the serpent's head from the rest of its writhing body. Thatcher dropped the bleeding head into the pond and collapsed into the shallows, exhausted. Looking lazily in the direction of the shot, he saw Matt, kneeling in the pool, wet from the battle and still holding a smoking rifle poised in his hands.

"Care to take that home for a souvenir, Professor?" asked Matt as he struggled to his feet.

"No, thank you," Schindler said breathlessly as he disentangled his arms from the serpent and lifted himself from the bloodstained waters. "Let's get out of this infernal place before history eats us alive."

Hayden sloshed over to where the others were standing from the water. He and Thatcher helped the professor up. "And let's do it as quickly as possible," he said. "Climb up to that large cave," he nodded to a cluster of cave openings on the wall of the cavern. He hefted his rifle again. "I'll cover your retreat." Hayden turned and instantly came face to face with a two-legged, raptor-like dinosaur about five feet tall. Opening his huge jaws the beast split the air with a horrific shriek.

"Run!" Matt shouted at the top of his lungs. Raising his rifle, he shot the reptile through its open mouth. Tripping backwards, the creature tumbled into the water. As Hayden turned instantly to retreat, another two-legged dinosaur stood in his way. He raised his rifle to fire, but the only return on his rifle was an audible click. His gun was empty. Without a pause, he grabbed the barrel of the weapon, wielding it like a club. The first full swing caught the unsuspecting beast squarely in the head, sending it splashing into the water.

Mike Thatcher and Professor Schindler stared at the big lizard that Hayden had just temporarily dispatched with his rifle. The creature thrashed momentarily in the water, attempting to stand. "Go, both of you!" Matt shouted. The two men stood and began to stumble through the water toward the caves. Hayden hurried to follow them when the raptor sprang up from the shallows, cutting him off again.

Thatcher and Schindler stopped to return. "Go!" Matt exploded. Before the word was out of his mouth, the beast had righted itself and stood to its full height. Hayden held up his rifle for another swing as the wary reptile bobbed and weaved with open jaws in preparation for the combat.

Glancing around him, Thatcher reluctantly backed away with Schindler. "Get me a rifle before that dinosaur kills him."

"Daptosaurus," corrected the professor as he watched the conflict in wonder.

Thatcher gave Schindler an incredulous look, but only for a split second. Reaching into the water, he snatched a large stick of wood and stepped toward Hayden and his assailant. But before he could help, another of the creatures suddenly sprang upon them snapping its jaws violently. Winding up, Thatcher smashed the beast in the face with all his strength.

Several feet away, Buck, Tom, and the others advanced back into the water to come to the aid of their comrades when three more of the two-legged predators confronted them. Drawing their rifles they began to fire aggressively, momentarily scattering the creatures. But like Matt, many of them also realized they'd run out of bullets. Their pockets held more ammunition, but the attacking raptors gave them little opportunity to reload. One by one, each of the hunters began beating away the attackers with the butts of their rifles as they became separated into smaller groups.

The hunting party was in full disarray.

In the center of the shallow pool, Hayden was now carrying on his battle with his raptor-like assailant single-handedly. Small in comparison with many of the other violent predators they'd met in the cavern, this creature was shrewder—and more threatening than the rest. For one thing, this monster had clawed hands and feet, which it wielded skillfully. And it had huge, plier-like jaws with large teeth. This was an attacking machine. However, it wasn't used to fighting a man with a gun—or even a club. With his next strike, Hayden took a swing at its legs, knocking it off its feet. When it quickly rose, Hayden went for its head again. But the small dinosaur learned quickly after the first three assaults and made adjustments. Blocking the hunter's next swing, the beast grabbed the rifle butt with its hands and almost ripped the weapon from Hayden's grasp. All the while, Matt had been backing to the nearest wall of the grotto, which was honeycombed with smaller caves. This was an unmatched battle and his opponent was quickly gaining the advantage. He needed to get to one of the small openings before the creature took control.

The raptor made one swipe with a claw, ripping through the sleeve of Matt's shirt. He winced at the stinging slit down his arm and only eluded the vicious jaws by doubling up and twisting away. This was his moment. With his last ounce of energy, he swung his rifle at the careless beast, connecting and sending him to the water. Losing his rifle, he ran three steps and dove into one of the small holes. The predator was not far behind. Snapping at his leg, the creature caught the sole of his boot. With one last, satisfying kick, Matt caught the beast full in the snout, freed himself, and disappeared into the cave.

Retreating from the shore of the pool, Tom, one other brave, and two of the ranchers were all battling with empty guns now. Slowly withdrawing from the open space of the grotto, they backed toward the wall of the cave where the largest tunnel yawned open to them, beckoning them to freedom and sanctuary.

Tom glanced behind him as they inched nearer to the cave. But the creatures were getting more aggressive, dodging in and out of formation and attempting to work their way around the men to cut off their retreat. "Break for the cave," he ordered, "all of you, while I hold them off. Go!" Advancing on the beasts with the sudden ferocity of a cornered wolverine, Tom took the raptors off guard. The three creatures stepped back in surprise, if only for a moment, while the gathered remains of the hunting party bolted for the cave opening. Still, the reptiles recovered quickly and with a vengeance. Leaping at Tom, they were on him in a heartbeat, their claws and open jaws making contact for the kill. Suddenly the report of a single gunshot resounded through the cavern. One of the raptors spun away from Tom and dropped dead, while the others backed away, regrouping for another attack. Tom rolled to his feet in a daze, holding his side where he had been pierced. In an instant one of the Indians and one of the ranchers crouched beside him. Struggling from the ground, the three of them scrambled for the opening with the reptiles in pursuit. They entered the cave on a dead run and collapsed to the rocky floor, five feet inside the mouth of the cave.

Looking up, Tom saw Hank, the ranch foreman, still holding his smoking rifle, which was trained on the cave entrance. "All I needed was a few seconds to reload," he smiled and lowered his gun. "And all I needed was one shot." He gestured to the cave entrance. "Look." Turning, the men on the ground squinted in disbelief at the mouth of the cave. There stood the two frustrated reptiles, bobbing, advancing, and then retreating at intervals—but neither of them daring to breach the barrier of the opening. "Mind you, I'm not complaining," the rancher shook his head, "but why don't they come any further?"

Tom smiled. "I think I know."

Thatcher and Schindler had been separated from the others during the attack of the raptors, or the Daptosauri as Schindler called them. It was all the same to Mike Thatcher. Schindler might have called them butterflies if he'd wanted to. Only two salient facts mattered to Thatcher: one of the creatures in question was pursuing them, and that creature wanted to eat them.

It was also significant to Thatcher that Schindler had found a good-sized stick with which he could help them to defend themselves. But the professor was not, by nature, a fighter. Even if he were, his battle with the snake had weakened him, severely limiting his defensive performance in any contest with a Daptosaurus.

"I'm pretty drained, Mike," he apologized as they faced the threatening beast with their crude weapons.

"That's okay, Joe," Thatcher reassured him. "He doesn't know that. Just stay close," he advised, "and look threatening."

Just then a shot rang through the cavern, diverting all their attention to a raised level, not far away. Schindler looked up quickly enough to see two men, dashing with Tom Running Wolf to the safety of a cave behind them—with two of the creatures in hot pursuit. As he did so, their own assailant refocused and made a lunge at them. Thatcher caught him in the side of his head with a roundhouse swing.

But Schindler continued to glance at the creatures on the level above them as they halted in their tracks at the cave entrance. Studying the scene, his face finally brightened. "Are you ready, Mike?" he announced as he took position. Without warning the professor drew his "club" back to pump and, with all his might, swung for the fences. He caught the surprised raptor on the forehead, sending him plummeting off balance to the ground in a tangle of arms and legs. "Let's go!"

Mike Thatcher was just as surprised as the Daptosaurus when Schindler turned and dashed for the caves with a limping sprint. But the rancher caught on fast, dropping his own stick and breaking for a large opening into the rock walls. He turned his head to see the two-legged beast standing and racing after them. Then, suddenly he cleared the threshold of the entrance just behind Schindler and stumbled to the cave floor. Only then did he turn to see what the others of the party, elsewhere, had already noticed. The creature had stopped at the cave opening as if forbidden by iron bars.

It was Buck's misfortune to have been abandoned in the cavern. In the first confusion with Schindler and the python attack in the shallow pool, Buck had dropped his camera at the water's edge to help rescue the professor. From there, everything had happened very quickly. The raid of the raptor pack took them all by surprise. Already separated, the party scattered like chaff in the wind. And despite their interest in each other's welfare, from that moment, survival in the grotto became, at best, a small group effort.

Initially when confronted by the raptors, Buck was with Tom Running Wolf and the other hunters. Like them, he'd tried to get back to Hayden, only to find that his friend had already been cut off. And with the beasts advancing on them, their only choice was reluctant retreat. It was then that he spotted his camera at the shoreline and, making a mad dash, snatched it up. Then, suddenly, he was alone, but not completely. One of the creatures was with him. And in marked contrast to the others, this reptile stood seven feet tall. Raising his rifle he shot at it wildly, missing it once and then hitting it in the leg. Roaring in pain, the beast turned aside momentarily. Bullets obviously had an effect. But with the third shot, Buck realized like the others that his gun was empty. Taking a desperate swing with the useless weapon he knocked the injured and off-balance predator to the ground and turned to run, but his options for escape were limited.

Running to the edge of the cavern he glanced back to see the creature stagger awkwardly to his feet and then, in renewed anger, search for his prey. Buck turned and began to climb the rock face behind him, struggling up the jagged ledges to a solitary opening, twenty feet over his head. He writhed upward, wincing each time his camera scraped against the rough rocks. Out of breath, he stopped climbing as he clung to the cliff. Regaining his strength he breathed deeply as he opened his eyes. Not far away, on the level ground, he searched the spot where his friends had been. Two raptors gathered around the mouth of a large cave and screeched in frustration. They stepped forward and backward at the gaping entrance, but would not enter.

Buck looked up. The inclined pathway to the cave was leveling off. Then he looked down. The raptor weaved impatiently at the base of the cliff, gurgling as it looked up at him. Then with a leap the creature began to climb toward him, finding footholds and grasping at crags with surprising agility.

"The cave," he thought. "That thing will stop at the cave." Digging his toes into the rocks, Buck churned his legs upward, only to slip and fall back down. His right foot struck the chin of the raptor, which opened his jaws to snap at him. The jagged teeth grazed the sole of his boot as he scrambled to get away. He frantically pulled his body up another several inches, and then several more. But the predator was also climbing in a crazed effort to overtake him.

"Get to the cave," he drove himself as his legs pushed him over the leveling rocks. The large mouth of the tunnel suddenly gaped before him. He worked himself to his feet and looked over his shoulder again. The raptor was starting to stand up on the incline leading to the opening. Without a pause, Buck threw himself forward, falling into the cave. Standing, he continued to stumble forward into the semidarknesss—and safety.

Chapter 10

THE LORD OF OSCURA MESA

Thatcher and Schindler sank in exhaustion to the floor against the wall of the cave. Panting and beyond conversation they lay there, drained of energy for several minutes. Thatcher opened his eyes and saw the Daptosaurus staring at them at the cave opening, fifteen feet away. He leaped to his knees as a sudden shot of adrenalin pumped through him. Staggering backwards, he fell against the cave wall again, breathless with renewed terror. But the creature only continued to pace in discontent at the threshold. He eyed him hungrily, but ventured no more than a few inches into the cave before pedaling back beyond its shadows. Finally the creature erupted with a single frustrated shriek, and backed away from the cave in disappointment.

"That's as far as they'll go," said the professor behind him. Thatcher turned to look at Schindler incredulously. "The Daptosaurus won't come into the caves." The professor laughed again and Thatcher joined him. Life seemed to flow into them as they paused to regain their strength. In the caves, they suddenly felt safe again.

"So," smiled Thatcher as he sat beside him on the cave floor, "your Diddlysaurus doesn't do caves either?"

"Daptosaurus," Schindler corrected him with a grin. "He was discovered about ten years ago up in Montana. His bones, I mean. He's what they call a dromaeosaurs, which means 'running lizard.' I've also heard him referred to as a raptor. He and his friends are carnivorous, fast, and intelligent." Thatcher glanced at the cave entrance again where the snarling beast still stood, weaving back

105

and forth in frustration. "Pound for pound," continued Schindler, "the Daptosaurus is possibly one of the most fearsome predators ever known. We're lucky to still be alive."

The professor pointed back into the huge chamber. "Life in that cavern, like any system of nature, operates under a highly developed social order, and the Daptosaurus are perfectly suited to it. They hunt in packs. They attack in a planned strategy. And they probably operate under the leadership of a dominant individual sometimes called an 'alpha.' The 'alpha' is usually older or larger, and has established his position at the top of the pecking order."

"All of these socially established behaviors keep that grotto in balance," Schindler continued. "Take our friend here for example. In that grotto, the Daptosaurus is on the top tier of the food chain. But throughout these caverns, the highest spot in this prehistoric social order seems to be occupied by the Nyah-Gwaheh."

The professor studied the creature at the cave entrance for several seconds. "I watched them as they pursued our company. None of those beasts will cross the threshold of these caves. And I believe the reason is that the Nyah-Gwaheh has established the barrier. Their boundaries are clear. It's our big bear's line in the sand so to speak."

Thatcher had been listening with interest. He took another look at the fierce creature barred from entrance at the mouth of the cave. "Supposin' one of those creatures crossed the barrier," Thatcher rubbed his chin. "Supposin' one of 'em challenged the dominance of your Nyah-Gwaheh?"

"It would throw the system into chaos. And nature is a house of order, not chaos. They wouldn't do that." He considered. "Well, it's possible the 'alpha' of these Daptosaurus could—and that might encourage others. But he'd have to be highly motivated, because any incursion into the domain of the Nyah-Gwaheh would have to be answered. Nature would require the Nyah-Gwaheh to re-establish his boundaries."

Buck lay breathless, inhaling the warm air of the cave as he recuperated. He closed his eyes and sighed with relief as he listened to the growls of his former attacker, twenty feet away at the entrance to the cave. With effort he forced himself to roll over and peer through the darkness to watch the killer.

The raptor stood before the cave entrance and straightened to its full stature. The beast's head bobbed and turned back and forth as it studied the entrance. The creature was cautious and at the same time calculating as it considered the cave. Buck could see the wheels turning behind those malevolent eyes, taking in all the data as an analytical mind seemed to be weighing options. Then, slowly, the creature seemed to make a decision as it narrowed its eyes to stare through the shadows at its prey—the lone man on the floor of the cave.

Anger, vengeance, and primitive determination had driven the raptor to challenge the status quo of his subterranean environment. Against all the rules of this primitive world, against all instinctive constraints, and against all natural fear—the raptor extended its neck and inserted its head into the cave entrance. As Buck locked eyes with the creature, he raised himself to his feet and backed falteringly beyond the light of the grotto. But the creature continued to stare in his direction as it stood motionless in the dark. And then, lifting its right foot, the beast took a tentative stride into the forbidden shadow of the cave itself. It paused again. Looking around, the lizard picked up its left foot and took another step past the inviolable threshold and froze, swiveling its head to take in all of the new surroundings. He had stepped outside of the grotto and into a new world.

Buck flattened his back against the far wall of the cave as the beast stretched its neck upward and adjusted its eyes, scanning the darkness in search of him. Then, in a sudden panic, Buck broke into a run. For the first few seconds Buck had the advantage of his adjusted vision. And the illuminated wall and ceiling of the cave gave him enough light to show him the way. Behind him he heard the creature bumping into walls and screeching as it knocked its head on the ceiling. But Buck never looked back.

The phosphorescent light began to dim ever so slightly as he got farther and farther from the underground grotto. Within minutes, the walls gave off only a faint light in the blackness. Buck was aware of running past side tunnels in the dark, and of his pursuer stopping to shriek down each one as he searched for his prey. The creature must have had a finely tuned sense of smell. In every instance the pause was only momentary before the killer was back on the scent and close behind.

Finally, the cave opened up into a vaulted cavern, thirty feet across. Buck passed an adjoining cave and decided to bypass it in favor of the larger passage in the obscurity. He realized his mistake immediately as the passage came to a dead end. He turned quickly to backtrack his way to the side passage. But the seconds he lost were seconds too late. Into the shadowed light of the cave raced his pursuer, who froze and narrowed its gaze on him. The chase was over. Buck retreated to the wall of the tunnel in terror as the Daptosaurus stood to its full height of seven feet and roared in triumph. Opening up its jaws, it leaped into the air and lifted its legs to impale its victim.

Suddenly, a huge blur from the adjoining side passage sprang from the shadows. With amazing agility and speed, the Nyah-Gwaheh caught the raptor mid-air with both forepaws, crushing the monstrous lizard to the ground. Recoiling with powerful legs and razor-sharp claws, the Daptosaurus kicked himself free of the armored bear and stood, facing the beast it had come to challenge.

Buck stood helplessly trapped in his corner of the cave and watched the savage contest with mingled terror and fascination. The formalities were instantaneous. The two creatures looked each other in the eye for a split second before the raptor took a snap at his opponent and backed away in the cramped space. Without hesitation, the Nyah-Gwaheh charged toward the retreating Daptosaurus when suddenly two additional raptors—also testing the order of nature—bounded into the fray, sinking their claws into the shoulder and ribs of the prehistoric bear. He reared up in pain as the alpha raptor, with a running start, also leaped into the air to dig his talons into the chest of his opponent.

The big lizards had scored with the initial assault and had drawn first blood. But the tough armor that protected the Nyah-Gwaheh made it difficult for the dinosaurs to do great damage with only their jaws and spiked teeth. Yet the advantages were even. The scales of the Daptosaurus made it equally difficult tor the Nyah-Gwaheh to claw the lizards with much effect. The bear knocked the raptor from his chest and managed to swat the others from his side.

No sooner had he batted them away than they surrounded him again for another coordinated assault. At once, the smaller dinosaurs attacked his flanks, while the larger creature leaped on his neck and sunk its teeth into the folds above his shoulders. With a full swing of his forelimb, the bear whacked one of the lizards off his leg, sending it dazed to the wall. But the agile creature righted itself instantly and hurled himself, feet-first, at the bear's head. The Nyah-Gwaheh quickly turned and crouched as the leaping dinosaur crashed into the larger raptor on his neck. Both tumbled to the ground, stunned.

The third lizard still clung to the bear's flank. Reaching back, the Nyah-Gwaheh grasped the beast with his forepaw, and flung him to the edge of the cave where Buck continued to stand, trapped against the wall, a captive audience of this savagery. Only now did the raptor notice the defenseless human. Opening his jaws, he struck out at Buck. But his attack was cut short as the Nyah-Gwaheh lunged out, grabbed the raptor by the neck, and, swinging him over his head like a dishrag, slammed him into the rocky cave floor. Releasing his grip, he dropped the raptor to the ground, limp and lifeless.

Seizing the moment, the other small Daptosaurus now leaped upon the bear's back, digging its claws and teeth into his spine. As the armored monster reared up in pain, the larger raptor was also upon him, gouging its claws into his exposed chest. Standing on his hind legs, the Nyah-Gwaheh roared in rage and fell, rolling onto his flank, crushing the remaining smaller beast.

Now on his back, the bear reached up with both forepaws and grabbed the remaining raptor by the head and rolled onto his stomach, pinning the creature like a wrestler. Holding the lizard's head in place, he growled as he looked into his face. Making eye contact, the Nyah-Gwaheh belched a terrific roar of anger into the air as he shoved the raptor's head up, exposing the undersurface of the neck and chest. The challenging Daptosaurus howled in momentary agony as the jaws of the armored bear clinched together. With a crunch of the breaking chest and spine, the raptor's body went limp and the cave fell again into silence.

With his back against the wall of the cave, only a few feet from the final death struggle, Buck stared at the scene, frozen in terrified amazement. Gradually the Nyah-Gwaheh lifted his eyes from his vanquished prey and looked directly at Buck. Focusing on the tiny human, he studied him curiously.

Trembling in breathless horror, Buck watched helplessly as the beast slowly lifted his foot from the dead raptor and reached toward him. Buck turned his head and clenched his eyes shut as the huge paw softly touched him and then powerfully pushed against his chest, literally pinning him to the wall of the vaulted cave. Gradually, Buck opened his eyes. The Nyah-Gwaheh stared at him, studying him intently as he began to breathe in a low growl.

After his escape from the creature in the grotto, Hayden had continued to crawl his way through the tiny passageway that had been his deliverance. When it eventually opened up into a tunnel he could stand up in, he had no reference of his whereabouts—or of the location of his friends. He was also now without a weapon. He called out in the dim light. "Buck! Professor! Thatcher! Tom!"

He was answered with silence and gloom. Disoriented and without a guide, his only recourse was to continue walking forward in what seemed to be another lava tube, taking him in one direction with few alternate routes. Within five minutes the natural phosphorescent light had vanished and he found it necessary to use his flashlight again. But within another ten minutes his surroundings began to resemble the cave closer to the surface with more outlets and options—and of course, more opportunities to get hopelessly lost.

Suddenly the ferocious roar of the Nyah-Gwaheh echoed through the cave in the distance. Matt stopped in his tracks. The instinct of the hunter kicked in. "Find your friends," he calculated. "Get your hands on a rifle again. Then renew the pursuit." He couldn't get this close and give up the hunt. Even without his rifle, his natural inclination was to find the creature. He began to walk again, quickening his pace, listening for another hint of direction. His mind and senses became totally focused on stalking the beast as he hurried down the corridor.

Then suddenly, a huge natural hole gaped open in his path, sinking deeper into the earth. He skidded to a halt, but still almost lost his balance at the lip of the pit. He grabbed onto a large stalagmite as one foot dangled into the hole. Holding firm to the anchor, he pulled himself upright. He took a deep breath, pointing his flashlight into the depths of the yawning chasm where the beam of light disappeared into the blackness.

As he steadied himself he noticed a rope wrapped around the stalagmite, trailing down the edge of the pit. Taking a closer look at the rope, he examined the base of the stone pillar. There on the ground was a sample bag with a curious yellow rock inside. He slipped the bag into his pocket as he glanced around the cave, searching the wall and floor. A few feet away lay a walking stick. He picked it up and began to examine the length of the wall beside it more intently

Walking along the cave he suddenly came to a stop as he shined the beam of his light onto the wall where several rocks had been chiseled away. Leaning the stick against the wall, he stooped to the floor and inspected the chips in the rock. Curious, he stopped for a closer examination, and looked up to consider, reacting with interest to what he'd found. As he ran his fingers over the cave floor beside the wall, he picked up another sample of the yellowish rock at his feet and studied it carefully.

At that moment a familiar voice spoke to him from behind. "That'll do, Hayden." Turning his head, Hayden could see Jeremy Webb armed with a pistol. "Now, stand up very slowly," continued Webb, "and face me."

Standing, Hayden turned to look at Webb. The Mammoth Steel executive wore a characteristic arrogant smile on his face. "You know, it's disappointing," he cocked his head to one side. "A famous hunter like yourself. And yet, all you've managed to catch so far is trouble. When I met you it was meddling. Yesterday, obstruction of justice. Today, trespassing. Who knows what tomorrow will bring,

Mr. Hayden? We've already arrested your little friend at the cave entrance. Snuck right up behind her. The redskin instinct isn't what is used to be."

Hayden stiffened as he clenched the yellow rock tighter in his fist. Webb didn't notice.

"But then again, your reputation has fallen a little short too, Mr. 'Bring 'em Back Alive.' Funny," Webb boasted, "so far I've managed to bring in more than you."

Hayden leveled his eyes squarely on Webb's. "You'd be surprised what I plan to bring in, Webb."

"Turn around and face the wall," Webb ordered. Giving Jeremy Webb one last, long look in the eye, Matt slowly turned his back on him. In the darkness he heard the man's footsteps in the gravel and rocks on the cave floor as he drew closer. Then he heard Webb cock his gun. Glancing to the wall, Matt eyed the walking stick he'd propped there only a minute ago.

Buck wanted to turn his gaze away, but found himself locked in the stare of the Nyah-Gwaheh, who continued to study him with a strange and curious fascination. The eyes of the creature moved as he examined the outline and the details of his captive, like a schoolboy observing a laboratory frog in a freshman science class. The contours of the bear-like face creased and wrinkled with primitive interest as he considered this odd little being who had invaded his world.

Buck tried to inhale, but could only fill his lungs partially against the pressure of beast's extended foreleg. He looked down and saw the bear's huge paw splayed across his entire chest, pressing him against the cave wall with incredible strength. The tendons of the massive foot stood out in muscular relief beneath the folds of armored skin. He carefully scrutinized the paw of the creature as a small pinprick of a needle appeared at the end of each toe. The toes gradually spread further apart by the seconds as each needle point grew into a claw—one, two, three inches long—and growing.

Buck took a quick glance into the face of the Nyah-Gwaheh, which was still growling—almost purring—and watching him with a certain awe. Then he looked back to the barbed toes, now nearly six inches long, which slowly began to turn inward. Intentionally or unintentionally, the needle-sharp spikes of the creatures paw sunk effortlessly through the fabric of Buck's jacket. In an instant, Buck felt the stab of those claws as each point pricked his skin and continued to drive deeper.

The sharp pain from the five wounds was almost unbearable. But Buck bit his lip, stifling any cry of anguish for fear of breaking the spell that seemed to enrapture the beast. Gritting his teeth, he squinted down at his own chest where blood was beginning to stain his jacket at the points pierced by the creature's claws. And still the claws sunk slowly deeper. The throbbing sting of pain was excruciating. He could bear it no longer as he screamed in agony, filling the caverns of Oscura Mesa with a torturous cry.

In the caverns, not far away, Webb and Hayden heard the scream in the darkness. Webb turned his head momentarily. That was all the time Hayden needed. Grabbing the walking stick at his elbow, he turned and swung it at Webb, clubbing the revolver from his hand. Before Webb could recover, Matt returned with a backhand swing, upper cutting his assailant on the side of the head, knocking him to the cave floor. Dropping the stick, Matt took one look in the darkness for the gun. His search was interrupted by another scream in the darkness.

Glancing up, and without another moment of hesitation, Hayden sprinted through the black tunnel in the direction of the cry. His flashlight gave him a dim pathway through the mountain, but he was still blind in the shadows. Then at once, he heard running footsteps. Almost instantly he crossed paths with Thatcher and Schindler through an adjoining cave. As they met, yet another cry echoed through the cave.

"Where did it come from?" shouted Hayden.

"This way," barked Thatcher, leading the way into another tunnel.

They had scarcely run fifty feet and turned a corner when they halted before a large vaulted room. The remaining four members of the hunting party were stopped at the entrance to the cavern, still and silent. Tom, his arms outstretched, stooped in front of the group, holding them back from any forward motion. Matt and his companions froze in their footsteps. It was a moment petrified in time like the rock walls that surrounded them.

There in the vaulted cavern, the Nyah-Gwaheh crouched as if poised for attack, with his front foreleg extended in front of him, his paw pinning Buck firmly against the cave wall. At the arrival of Matt and the others, the creature erupted with a deep guttural growl as his lips curled into a snarl. He eyed the growing group of intruders with suspicion as he glanced between them and his captive prey. Buck stood against the rocks, held in place by the powerful paw, and the piercing claws, which had already sunk into his chest. Blood from the five wounds stained his jacket in growing blotches of red as Buck endured the stinging pain in silent agony.

Thatcher drew his rifle to fire. Hayden and Schindler both stopped him. "Hold your fire," Matt warned.

"Well, we can't just let him bleed to death," argued Thatcher in frustration.

"One sudden move from us and he'll tear Buck to pieces," answered Schindler. "Isn't that right, Matt?"

But Hayden wasn't listening. He thought as he studied the flash camera dangling at Buck's side. "Professor, the bear's eyes," he asked. "Are they sensitive to light?"

"Very," Schindler answered him. "His habits are completely nocturnal."

Hayden slowly edged his way to the front of the small group. As he did so, the low growl of the beast grew louder. Matt stopped, sank to the ground and settled into a crouch. "Buck," he said softly.

Buck appeared almost lifeless, held against the wall with his eyes clenched shut. "Buck," Matt repeated. His friend opened his eyes and looked languidly at him. "Is the flash on your camera connected?" he asked.

The captive man paused for a moment and then slowly nodded his head.

"Can you lift the camera with your right arm?" Matt continued.

Considering, Buck gave the request a trial, lifting his right arm only an inch or two, before letting it settle to his side. He nodded again.

"Then do exactly as I say," Hayden counseled. "Reach slowly down with your right hand and get a good hold on the camera."

Following Matt's directions, Buck moved his hand, inch by inch, to the camera at his side. As he did so the creature began to growl, and then to snarl, curling his lips away from his sharp, white teeth. Buck clenched his eyes shut again in pain. Hayden slowly waved the others gently back to the wall of the cave. The counterbalance of the retreating men mollified the beast just enough as his teeth and snarl disappeared, but the growl continued.

"Now," whispered Hayden, "close your grip on the handle and the shutter." Buck responded, following the instructions to the letter.

"Good," he commended. "Now, open your eyes again and look at me." Buck opened his eyes with a shallow breath and fixed his gaze on his friend. "Okay," he instructed, "when I give you the signal . . ."

At that instant Jeremy Webb rounded the corner of the tunnel. His head was bleeding and his eyes bitter with rage. He set his jaw and took dead aim at Hayden. Buck saw him and blurted out in pain. "Matt!"

Matt jerked his head around to spot Webb out of the corner of his eye. His reaction was instinctive and instantaneous, tumbling to the ground as Webb pulled the trigger. The bullet whizzed by him, striking the Nyah-Gwaheh in the front leg. Both stung and startled by the shot, the enraged animal reared up with a maddened roar and descended, prepared to impale his captive victim with both claws.

Twisting forward, Matt screamed at the top of his lungs. "Now, Buck!"

Jerking the camera upward, Buck thrust it toward the face of the enraged beast, turned his head and fired the flash. With an ear-splitting roar, the Nyah-Gwaheh stumbled backward, groping in the air.

Terrified, Jeremy Webb backed away and disappeared into the darkness as the entire cave erupted into confusion.

Buck tried to take a step from the wall, but haltingly collapsed to the floor of the cavern. Seizing the moment, Hayden dodged the floundering forepaws of the blinded beast as he rushed forward to his friend. "Come on, buddy," he said, lifting Buck to his feet and dragging him across the vaulted room to the tunnel. All the while, the others covered the rescue with gunfire. Some of the bullets stung the creature while others only glanced off his scaled armor with little effect other than to further infuriate him.

Matt was almost to the tunnel when the monster staggered toward him. "Get out!" he screamed to the others as he and Buck sidestepped the bear. Immediately the blinded Nyah-Gwaheh swung a huge paw in his direction. Hayden jerked Buck from the path of the beast, and the two of them tumbled to the ground.

"Umph," Buck winced in agony as he muffled a cry. "Good grief, Matt," Buck grumbled in an undertone, "he's blind—not deaf."

"He's not even blind for long," muttered Hayden as he watched for the beast to turn from them. "Let's go," Matt nodded. Lifting Buck to his feet, Matt stumbled with him to the cavern exit, where the rest of the company still stood, firing their weapons. "What are you waiting for?" He shouted at them. "Get out!" Again the creature spun in the direction of the noise. Backing away from the advancing Nyah-Gwaheh, they all turned and began to run, followed by Matt and Buck.

Entering the darkness of the narrower caves, the few men who still had flashlights turned them on. Thatcher and Schindler led the way. But the professor, quickly exhausted by the pace, soon slowed to a limping run and faltered. "Joe." Thatcher grabbed him and hobbled forward under his weight.

Tom and the others caught up with them and hesitated. "Go on," Tom shouted at his comrades and took Schindler by the opposite arm to steady him. "Here, Mike," he said as he helped Thatcher carry him forward. "Professor, we can do this." Thatcher responded.

"Thanks Tom," Schindler sighed in painful exhaustion and quickened his pace. The cave entrance couldn't be far away.

Meanwhile, only footsteps behind them, Matt and Buck were struggling to keep up and to distance themselves from the angry terror they had eluded in the arched cavern. Gradually Matt slowed to a walk. "Hold up, Buck," Hayden paced them. "How are you doing?"

Buck nodded. "It hurts to walk. But I'm alive."

The muffled growl of the Nyah-Gwaheh thundered far away in the recesses of the caves, giving every indication that the blinded beast remained where they had left him. "We might be safe now," Hayden glanced down the cave. "I think we hurt his eyes. He's probably still groping in that cavern." Suddenly a ferocious roar pierced the air, booming through the tunnels.

Without hesitation, Matt and Buck together broke into a stumbling run. "Looks like he found his way," panted Hayden.

"And his eyesight," agreed Buck.

Instantly, another bellowing roar reverberated in the caves behind them, this time much closer. "Keep going," Matt encouraged breathlessly. They were running at their full capacity now, alone in the caverns with a monster gaining ground on them. Buck tripped on a crag at his feet and the two of them almost went down. But Hayden pulled him up as they faltered forward. And they continued to run.

Their muscles stung with fatigue. Their mouths were dry. Their lungs ached with each breath of the stifling air. They were involuntarily slowing down. Exhausted, their physical bodies had given all they had to give. Yet another roar, much closer now, reminded them of their imminent peril. They forced themselves forward a few more awkward steps. And then, turning a bend in the cave, they saw it. Daylight! A hidden reserve of energy pumped into their veins as they pushed themselves toward the illumination, which meant life. Treading with agonizing effort the two drove their footsteps, one ahead of another until suddenly they burst into the air—and the light of the sun.

Chapter 11

INTO THE DAYLIGHT

Lilia sat helplessly behind a truck on the valley floor where she had
been detained by the miners a half hour ago. She cursed herself
silently for allowing the men of Mammoth Steel to slip behind her
on the ledge and catch her unaware. It had been careless and stupid.
For over a thousand years that overlook had never been taken by an
invading force. Now, under her watch, it had fallen and she had been
taken captive.

In Lilia's defense, the company engineers had been busy the day
before. On that first day they had begun to survey and excavate an
alternate access way to the cave on the blind side of the mountain
ledge. Comprising little more than a graded pathway to a clearing just below the shelf and a ladder scaling the remaining fifteen
feet, the new access provided a more convenient access to the cave
entrance than the antiquated steps. But as a benefit, it also seriously
undermined the strategic integrity of the ledge against attack. No
single defender could have now protected the left flank of the shelf.
But even knowing that, Lilia could hardly have been comforted. The
men had taken her completely off guard and overwhelmed her. Then
she had been forced to watch as a demolition crew hauled stacks of
explosives to the cave entrance, in preparation to desecrate the holy
mountain of Oscura Mesa beyond redemption.

She remembered with seething anger Jeremy Webb's arrival at the
scene of conquest. Stepping over the barrier into the clearing, he'd
chuckled as he haughtily faced her. "Well, you're no Geronimo, Miss

118

Bluelake," he gloated. The other miners laughed irreverently as he turned and approached the cave itself.

"Ford," he snapped.

The big foreman had just climbed over the lip of the clearing with a spool of wire. "Yeah, what is it?"

"Get the girl out of here, and keep an eye on her," he ordered. "We'll decide what to do with her later. Meanwhile, get this stuff ready to close the entrance."

"You'll be sealing ten men inside," she said gravely.

Webb, smiled. "Yes, I know," he said. "Ten men and one god."

Turning from Lilia as dismissively as if she didn't exist, he spoke to Ford. "I'm going in to check one thing out," he said, taking out a revolver and spinning the chamber before putting it back in his holster. "I shouldn't be long." Then he disappeared inside the cave.

Up to this point, Lilia had observed the sacrilegious behavior of these men and the conquest of the ledge with a passionless detachment that surprised and at the same time disappointed her. That she could witness the seizing of the last religious remnant of her people with such an absence of feeling struck her to the core. That she could anticipate the impending demolition of the cave, or even the cold-blooded murder of her friends inside, with such a hopeless and impassive disconnect showed her how cynical she had truly become. She shook her head in self-reproach.

But as she watched the entrance of Jeremy Webb into the sacred cave, Lilia was overwhelmed with an uncontrollable feeling of instant revulsion. No other desecration of this hallowed ground had touched her soul with such loathing. The thought of Webb treading into that holy place where her grandfather's footsteps had walked only a day before filled her with an abhorrence that she was unable to conceal.

Tearing her eyes from the cave she realized that Ford had been watching her. The expression of grief on her face had unnerved him. "Get her out of here," he bellowed, and instantly a miner grabbed her by the arm and jerked her toward the edge of the shelf.

"Fitch, you ready with that coil?" he growled to another miner.

"Yeah," answered Fitch, scooping up a spool of wire that was hooked in a complex netting of lines to the crates at the cave entrance.

"I was just going to double check all the caps and connections here before I went down."

"We'll take care of that," Ford grumbled. "You just get down there and be ready for detonation. We should blast in just a few minutes—as soon as Webb comes out of that cave."

Ford began to walk away when something caught his attention. Turning, he snatched something from the base of the altar. As Ford held it chest high, Lilia recognized Hayden's tranquilizer rifle. Opening the two large barrels he looked at it, examined the cartridges, and closed it again. "And you," he gestured to a short man about to leave the ledge with Fitch. "Take this with you," he took a long look at the double-barreled gun and smiled before tossing it to him. "Put it in my truck for me. I just got a new rifle."

Led by Fitch, who carefully unrolled the spool of wire down the mountain, the men dragged Lilia over the edge of the canyon shelf and began to descend the stairway to the base of the rocky ravine. Lilia looked out over the floor of the valley, now covered with the scattered debris of occupation. Mammoth Steel had taken full possession of the Tonowa land, defacing the quiet beauty of the Canyon de Dios with trucks and mining equipment. They had staked their blasphemous claim of ownership by right of legal decree and the might to enforce it.

But the entitlement to the Garden of the Gods was not for any man to give or take. She suddenly knew that now. In spite of the implements of industrial destruction—which littered the canyon floor—in spite of the imminent demolition of the ledge and of the altar held sacred for a thousand years, and in spite of Jeremy Webb's irreverent footsteps violating the pathway of the hallowed cave of her people, something spoke peace to her soul that greater powers than man's were still at work and in control in the Vega Towachi.

Lilia was lost in her thoughts as the two miners marched her down the steps and across the floor of the canyon to the edge of the cornfield where a command post had been set up and a myriad activities were underway. She watched as the short miner propped the tranquilizing rifle beside a crate of supplies while Fitch continued to unroll the spool of wire into the site and set it down. "You watch the girl," he ordered one of the men who had brought her down the canyon wall. Picking up a red flag from the ground, he tossed it to the short miner. "You clear the area."

"Ford said to put this rifle in his truck," the man argued.

"He also said get ready to blast," Fitch answered back. "Now forget the rifle and clear the area or somebody's gonna get killed." The miner hesitated briefly. "Now!" shouted Fitch, and the man picked up the red flag and ran from the area. Fitch continued to mutter to himself and to the other miner as he stooped to cut the wires from the spool and began to connect them to a plunge detonator. "That fool Ford has packed that cave with enough TNT to pulverize half the mountain."

Ford had waited for more than a half an hour for Webb to return from the depths of the mountain. Suddenly, Webb stumbled in exhaustion to the cave mouth and collapsed at the entrance, clinging to the rocks at the threshold. Breathlessly, he looked around as his eyes adjusted to the light. "Ford!" he shouted at the top of his lungs.

"Yeah, what are you screaming about?" asked the foreman. He stood at the edge of the landing, supervising two other miners as they spliced some wires together. "What took you so long in there?"

"That's my business," said Webb, shaking the darkness from his head as he stepped away from the cave. "Are those explosives in place?"

Ford walked over to him. "Ready and waiting," he said as he pointed to two stacks of crates labeled "TNT" standing on either side of the cave entrance. The ledge was littered with other emptied boxes, wire spools, and blasting equipment that had been hastily carried there and abandoned.

Ford smiled. "Did you find what you were looking for?"

"I know what I need to know," said Webb soberly. "Now get down to the canyon floor. It's time to end this." Walking purposefully to the edge of the shelf he cupped his hands around his mouth and shouted. "Clear this mountain!" he announced in warning. "Prepare to blast!"

Ford hurried from the ledge, passing Clark Simmons of the Interior Department as he arrived in concern at the edge of the shelf. He hurried onto the clearing as other miners brushed past him, evacuating the area. "Webb," he stood officiously, "I thought we agreed to use high explosives here only as a last resort."

Webb grabbed Simmons by the collar, screaming into his face. "This is a last resort!"

"But there are people in there," Simmons stuttered.

Sneering, Webb angrily threw the federal representative to the ground and pointed into the cave. "He's in there, you stupid idiot!" Stepping over Simmons, Webb leaned across the low lip at the edge of the clearing and screamed again. "Prepare to blast!" With a final contemptuous look at Simmons, Webb climbed over the wall and down the steps. Simmons hurriedly followed him.

Rushing down the canyon steps, the two of them were on the floor of the valley within a few minutes. Once on level ground, Webb sprinted to a spot at the side of the cave on the mountain, well clear of the range of the planted TNT. A group of miners, including Ford and the demolition crew, waited for him. Webb stopped, out of breath, and observed the detonating wires stringing off a good deal farther. Simmons arrived, exhausted, a moment later.

"Give me that bullhorn," he barked, and Ford hurriedly tossed him a handheld megaphone. The device squealed as he put it to his mouth, and then his distorted voice boomed through the area. "Take cover everyone! You have five seconds to vacate the blast perimeter." He barely waited three. "Detonate!" he shouted and stooped behind a boulder for cover.

Lilia watched with interest as Fitch finished his work. Not far away she heard the voice of the short miner, "Clear the area," he shouted. "Clear the area." She looked up to see him waving the red flag and continuing to shout his warning as Mammoth employees scurried from the blast zone at the base of the mountain.

"Prepare to blast!" she heard another voice shout, this time more frantically, from the canyon wall. Looking up, she saw Jeremy Webb leaning over the natural barrier of the ledge. He then climbed over the lip and quickly moved two steps at a time down the rock stairway. He was followed by Simmons and several others.

Lilia looked back to Fitch as he double-checked the connections on the detonator and stood, placing both hands on the plunger. She continued to glance between the detonator and the cave entrance on the wall above. "Hurry, Matt," she whispered under her breath. She took a wide look around. All eyes of the command post, including those of her guard, were on Webb and those who followed him as they reached the canyon floor and raced for cover almost one hundred feet from them. She backed away from the distracted miner, toward the tranquilizer rifle, still leaning on the crate a step away.

Suddenly she heard the voice of Jeremy Webb, shouting over a bullhorn. "Detonate!" Without a pause, Lilia grabbed Matt's rifle by the barrel and swung with all her might. She caught her guard in the back of the head and dropped the weapon as he toppled to the ground. Before the rifle was clear of her fingers, Lilia was already bolting into a dead sprint toward Fitch whose hands were poised on the plunge detonator. Tucking her neck like a fullback, she buried her head into the man's midriff as the two of them toppled over into the sand and dirt, knocking the detonator over with them.

"I said detonate!" screamed the angry amplified voice of Webb. But Lilia was only vaguely aware of it, locked in a deadly wrestling match with Fitch. Pushing her away, he righted the detonator again. Lilia dove for the wires on the ground, and with the strength she had left, she ripped the lines from the plunger, just as Fitch thrust it downward. No explosion followed as Fitch threw himself to the ground, struggling with Lilia for the disconnected cables.

"Detonate!" bellowed the voice of Webb. "De-ton-ate!"

Inside the cave, the small group of hunters was stumbling toward the light. Two ranchers and an Indian burst into the day first. Turning back inside, they encouraged their friends behind them to hurry. An instant later, Tom and Thatcher emerged from the cave with Schindler between them. They stopped, closed their eyes, and breathed in the fresh air of the desert with quiet gratitude.

Suddenly an amplified garble of words reached their ears from the valley floor. The tangle of syllables paused for a heartbeat. Then one word tore through any peace remaining of their moment in the sunlight. "Detonate!" came the raspy sound of a voice through a bullhorn. In an instant, the men looked at the debris on the ledge, the crates of TNT stacked against the walls of the cave, and the multiple wires leading from the boxes over the edge of the shelf.

"Quickly," yelled Schindler, "get out! Now!"

Scrambling in pandemonium over the edge, the men disappeared down the stairway. Thatcher stopped at the wall and glanced back to the cave. "What about Hayden and Buck?" Schindler paused and ran back up to join Thatcher when another amplified announcement chilled his heart. "I said detonate!" shouted the harsh voice, distorted with anger. "Detonate!" the scream blared out again. "De-ton-ate!"

Schindler looked painfully at Thatcher as they both realized there was nothing they could do if they hoped to save their lives. In an agonizing split second decision, they both fled from the ledge, leaving their two friends behind in the cave.

Struggling on the ground, Fitch and Lilia wrestled for the disconnected cables. Lilia clenched her fists around the wires and tucked her arms into her body in a desperate effort to hang on to them. Unable to loosen her grasp from behind, Fitch threw his arm around her neck and began to strangle her in the crook of his elbow. Choking, Lilia slowly unfolded her arms and groped at Fitch's stranglehold. But as he reached his free arm around her to grab the lines, Lilia swung back with her free elbow, jabbing Fitch in the gut. He instantly doubled in pain as Lilia staggered to her feet.

Looking around to get her bearings, she saw, one hundred feet away, Webb and Ford running toward her. She glanced from them to the canyon wall. There on the stairway were the members of the hunting party. She thought she could see Tom Running Wolf. Just above him she recognized Thatcher and Schindler climbing from the ledge. They had to hurry. She opened her mouth to call to them but before the words were out of her mouth, Fitch tackled her to the ground. His hands wrapped around hers, groping for the precious wires. And then other hands took her by the arms, while still others pried open her fingers and ripped the lines from her grasp. She fought to get up but was thrust violently to the dirt.

She looked up to see Jim Ford standing over her. Planting his boot heavily on her shoulder, he pinned her to the ground with a cruel sneer. A few feet away, Fitch was hurriedly stripping the wires as Webb dropped his bullhorn and kicked it out of the way. Grabbing the plunge detonator on the ground, he propped it upright. "Hurry with that," he shouted with nervous agitation as Fitch fumbled with the lines.

Lilia wrenched her head around to look for her friends. They had arrived at the floor of the valley and were running for protection from the explosion they knew was imminent. But where was Matt? At that instant a low rumble shuddered from the cave, turning her blood cold. In a split second the growl erupted into an angry roar. Reverberating from the depth of the mountain, it rolled down from the canyon wall and tumbled like a tidal wave out onto the valley floor. Ford looked up, took his booted foot from her shoulder, and backed away. Fitch paused in his work and twisted his head to squint in the direction of the cave. Jeremy Webb froze in horror.

"Hurry," yelled Webb in a panic. Fitch didn't need to be told. Struggling desperately to attach the spliced wires to the detonator, his trembling fingers scrabbled nervously with the wing nuts at the connection posts.

Lilia peered up at the ledge on the canyon wall. As her eyes focused on the sacred shelf, she suddenly saw Matt, with his friend Buck, struggling over the barrier of the ledge, just as another roar, this time much louder, echoed from the cave. Rolling to her left she reached for the bullhorn on the ground, drew it to her mouth, and pulled the trigger—just as Fitch threw his hands from the detonator wires and shouted, "Detonate!"

"Matt," Lilia screamed. "Jump! Juuump!"

Even as Lilia shouted those words, Jeremy Webb grit his teeth and thrust down on the detonator.

Matt and Buck emerged into the light of day in an awkward run. They stumbled past the crates of explosives and the rubbish left by the detonation crew, hardly aware of any reality but their escape from the cave. They fell to the ground when a single growl echoed from the cave and rose into a full roar that might have been heard for miles. Pushing themselves to their feet again they staggered to the short barrier wall and began to climb over the lip of stones that fringed the ledge. Another roar belched from the cave. Hayden barely glanced back as he pulled Buck over the barrier and steadied him on the top step of the canyon stairway. He hadn't yet turned to descend the stairway when a distorted but familiar voice rang in his ears. "Matt," he heard Lilia's frenzied voice over a gravelly megaphone. "Jump! Juuump!"

In that instant the Nyah-Gwaheh burst from the broad mouth of the cave in all his ferocity. Flanked on each side by the crates that lined the cavern entrance, he paused, flinching at the brilliant sunlight as he bellowed forth a roar that shook the mountain.

Hayden's reaction was instinctive—and instantaneous. Grabbing Buck by the arm, he pulled him toward the end of the stairway to the left of the shelf. Buck, following Matt's lead, churned his feet into the rocks of the top step and the two of them leaped to a drop of ten feet or so and then toppled down the craggy slope. But even as they tumbled downward, a deafening explosion propelled immense shocks through the earth and sky. Debris was already raining down everywhere as they crawled to a rock outcropping that shielded them from what seemed like an avalanche bringing half the mountain crashing around them.

The pandemonium of falling rocks and the trembling of the earth seemed to last for several minutes. Their eyes stung and their lungs burned as the suffocating dust from the explosion and the landslide surrounding them, threatening to crush them where the falling earth itself had not succeeded. Coughing and choking, they covered their faces with the collars of their shirts as they groped their way through the powdered earth, which hung in the air like a fog at the edge of night.

Below and to the left of the demolished ledge, Hayden finally staggered onto the new approach that the Mammoth engineers had begun to etch into the canyon wall the day before. Only a hint of the clearing below the shelf remained. A light wind like the heat from a furnace rose up from the floor of the canyon, dissipating the dust and allowing them to at least see—and breathe.

Looking up through a clearing in the thick vapor of pulverized earth, Matt squinted at the revered shelf, where rocks were still spilling off the edge. There, over the brink, hung the armor-skinned foreleg of the Nyah-Gwaheh, its open paw reaching out into the air—as if grasping for life. Silent as the stifling heat, which burned down upon the crushed mountain, the razor claws of the beast extended outward, inches from each toe, lifeless and still.

Chapter 12

RAMPAGE AND REVENGE

The enormous fireball that exploded from the cave—engulfing the mountainside in fire, smoke, and destruction—had lasted no more than a few seconds. In its wake the monster on the ledge disappeared in a cloud of dust and rocks as half the canyon wall disintegrated and rained down on the slopes and the valley below.

In the camp, scores of miners and other workers had been watching—thinking themselves beyond the limits of the blast perimeter. In an instant, any false thoughts of security vanished in a blast of violent flames as they ran for their lives or dove for protection under vehicles and mining equipment. Suddenly the entire area resembled a war zone. The pulverized debris of the explosion hung suspended in the air, blending with the desert heat to create an unbreathable miasma of palpable haze.

Gasping and hacking, Webb staggered through the smog, squinting to see anything through the settling dust. Gradually, he began to make out the devastation of the explosion. But all that mattered as he looked to where the cave had been, was the massive mound of rock that covered the remains of the shelf—and the single motionless paw reaching into the empty air over the edge.

"Whoa!" he cheered from the pall of dust and smoke. "We got him!" he shouted in triumphant exultation. "We got him!"

One by one, other miners responded to the announcement and joined their voices in the victorious shouts. Within seconds a chorus

128

of Mammoth Steel employees were one in enthusiastic applause of their united accomplishment. The Nyah-Gwaheh was dead.

In the midst of the jubilant cheers of the triumphant miners, Matt and Buck stumbled through the fragments of rock and the remnants of the access path. Still coughing and wiping the dust from their eyes, they arrived at the valley floor where Thatcher, Schindler, and the survivors of the hunting party anxiously met them.

"Matt! Buck!" the relieved professor cried out. "Thank heavens you're alive!"

Hayden merely nodded, but said nothing as he shook the dust from his hair and his shirt. "Take care of Buck," he said with firmness as he strode resolutely away from them. None of them moved as they watched him walk in the direction of the mining command post.

Webb and the miners were still wildly congratulating themselves as Hayden approached. Their elation subdued only slightly as the hunter marched through their midst to Lilia, who was sitting up in the dirt, rubbing her arm. Hayden stooped to the ground on one knee. "Are you okay?" he asked her.

"I'm all right," she answered. "You and Buck?"

"We're alive—barely."

Looking up, they were in the center of a sea of men. All around them, most of the miners were still chuckling and backslapping in euphoric celebration. And most of the participants were oblivious to them until Jeremy Webb strutted near and stood over them. "Boys, let me introduce you to Mr. Matt Hayden, who almost always brings 'em back alive. Well, today hasn't been one of his better days. I'd suggest you take a page from our book, Hayden." Grinning, Webb pointed up to the shattered ledge where a prehistoric beast lay buried under tons of rock. "Because that's how we hunt!"

Webb burst into a roar of laughter and his men joined in. Without warning, Hayden bolted upward, thrusting his fist squarely into Webb's face. Webb's laughter ceased abruptly as he tumbled to the ground. Several nearby miners grabbed Hayden and restrained him while others helped their boss to his feet. "You could have killed us, you maniac," Matt shouted madly as he fought to free himself of their grasp. "But then again, I think that was your intention. And I'm still not sure why. Is it just greed and power Webb? Or is there something else up in that cave?"

Webb stood unsteadily and shook off the hands that had supported him. A tiny track of blood trickled from his mouth. He touched the blood with his fingers and looked at it. Lifting his eyes, he glared at Hayden, still held firmly by the other miners. Webb came close, staring grimly into Matt's face. The laughter had disappeared, but a thin smile crept slowly across his lips. "What was up there in the cave," hissed Webb, "is dead. We took care of it our way." Backing away a step, Webb took off his windbreaker. "And we can take care of you too."

Drawing back his fist, Webb punched Hayden in the stomach, then in the face, and again in the stomach. Matt doubled over. "Matt," Lilia cried out from the edge of the growing crowd where she was also detained.

Webb reached down, grabbed Hayden by the collar, and jerked him upright. "I warned you to stay out of this, Hayden. I told you to get out. I even offered to pay you to leave. Now it's time for you to pay."

As Hayden looked up to stare Webb coldly in the eye, frantic shouts echoed form the base of the wall. "Run," came the scattered voices. "Look out! Run!" Webb furrowed his brow and jerked his head around to look up at the canyon ledge. Hayden, weakened from his beating, turned more slowly.

On the floor of the valley, ranchers and miners alike were running from the base of the canyon wall, shouting in frenzied shock as they pointed behind them to the ledge. From the demolished shelf, where half the mountain seemed to have settled, small rocks and chunks of debris were beginning to fall haphazardly down the slope. The mound of fallen rubble quivered almost imperceptibly and yet unmistakably. And then, the huge paw of the beast flexed. Opening outward, the huge claws retracted as the toes balled into an armored fist and withdrew slowly beneath the wreckage of rock. Momentarily, all was still and silent again.

Suddenly the mound of fallen rock violently exploded upward as the Nyah-Gwaheh burst from the tomb of mountain debris. Large pieces of rock showered down the sides of the canyon and upon the camp below as miners fled before the horror. Flinching in the sunlight, the creature stood on his hind legs and belched out a roar that thundered from one end of the valley to the other. Without an instant of hesitation, the furious bear settled on all fours and crawled from the ledge toward the men in the canyon.

Webb and the other miners of Mammoth Steel loosened their hold on Hayden and scattered in terror. Momentarily weakened, Matt tumbled to the ground, but Lilia was there in a heartbeat to help him to his feet. He nodded to her in appreciation. "Let's get out of here."

Lilia led the way, holding Matt up by his arm and then suddenly stopped. "Wait!" she said, her face lighting up. Turning, Lilia ran over to the empty clearing where Matt's tranquilizing rifle still lay in the dirt. He brightened as he watched her pick it up. "You're gonna need this," she said, tossing it to him.

Catching it, he held his gut, winced, and shook off the beating. "That's what we came for," he smiled. "Come on." The two of them ran haltingly off in search of safety.

But they didn't get far. By this time the Nyah-Gwaheh had reached the floor of the canyon. Standing on his hind legs he erupted with another resonating roar, lighted down on all fours, and began to lope forward—in Matt and Lilia's direction. The two of them had not yet found a suitable hiding place. "Quick," shouted Matt, pointing to a nearby semi-truck trailer. "Get under there." Piled high with rails for mining car tracks, the trailer was not only heavily armored, but also hunched low to the ground under tons of steel hardware. Sprinting to the trailer, they both crawled underneath for its meager offering of safety.

Meanwhile, Webb, Ford, and several other miners had taken refuge among crates of mining hardware, heavy equipment, and stacks of lumber. Not far away, two company dump trucks were parked. Fitch licked his lips nervously as he took a few quick glances between the trucks and the monster. "You said the explosives and the landslide would kill it, Webb. What happened?"

Webb shook his head. "It was tougher than I thought," he said. "But that doesn't mean it can't be killed. Everything can be killed."

"Not me," Fitch shot back in agitation. "I'm not ready to be killed. Not yet."

"Calm down and keep your head," growled Webb, "or that monster will tear it from your body."

"Not if I'm not here," he screamed to Webb. "And I'm not gonna wait for him to find me." Impulsively, Fitch bolted away toward the trucks, a hundred feet away.

"Fitch," yelled Webb. But he was gone. "Stupid, crazy fool!" he grumbled.

Now Webb could only watch as Fitch sprinted for the first truck. But the sudden movement attracted the eye of the creature. With a tremendous roar, he bounded toward the trucks to cut the man off. Within twenty feet of Fitch, the beast took one carefully timed leap as he raised his right paw. Then with one powerful stroke, the Nyah-Gwaheh caught Fitch mid-stride and hurled him like a beanbag through the air and into the wall of the canyon where he fell to the ground in a lifeless heap.

Turning, the creature squinted his eyes across the floor of the desert, looking for more movement. His eyes were getting more comfortable with the sunlight as he scanned the camp in search of his tiny prey.

Several of the miners had taken refuge among stacks and stacks of thick bracing lumber, arranged like a patchwork of wooden towers on the valley floor. Spotting them, the beast roared and loped over to the checkerboard of pylons, while the men scrambled in and out of the wide corridors like rats in a maze. Meanwhile, a dozen other miners gathered at the edge of the wood stacks, positioned for an assault with larger caliber firearms. As their fleeing comrades darted past, the riflemen suddenly emerged from their place of protection to engage the beast point blank. Flinching in the barrage of bullets, the creature backed away.

Under the flatbed trailer, Matt grabbed his tranquilizer and crawled from his hiding place. "This is my chance," he told Lilia. "Wish me luck."

"Be careful," was all that Lilia said as Matt stole away.

Nearing the distracted beast, whose back was still to him, Hayden leveled both barrels at the back of the creature and pulled the trigger. What he heard was an audible click—but that was all. Stepping back, he opened up the rifle and looked into the chambers. Both chambers were empty.

Hayden looked up again to see the Nyah-Gwaheh halt in his retreat from the rifle-packing miners. And then he charged at them. As the men sought cover behind the high stacks of timber, the Nyah-Gwaheh fell with a roar against the heavy beams. One by one, the towers of wood toppled like a line of dominos, crushing the men who had sought refuge there.

Two of the men emerged between the toppling stacks. Running through the ruin of lumber, they sprinted behind the creature, and past Hayden, who looked up from his empty weapon into the face of the angry Nyah-Gwaheh. In a beat, Matt turned on his heels and broke into a sprint, catching up to the men with the beast just behind him. Arriving at the semi-trailer just ahead of the creature, the three of them dove underneath.

"You brought company," Lilia remarked.

"We won't be staying long," said one of the miners as he sprawled on his belly as far from the beast as possible.

"We're heading for one of those," said the other man behind him, pointing to two company dump trucks just fifty feet away.

But Lilia was hardly listening. The single-minded Nyah-Gwaheh was already peering underneath the trailer, snarling aggressively. "Matt," she asked curiously, "what happened to 'the big sleep'?"

Hayden gestured to the rifle he'd dropped at his feet. "The chambers are empty," he said in frustration. "Where are the cartridges?"

Lilia thought. "Ford, the foreman," she suddenly realized. "He was looking it over. He had to have taken them."

Attracted by her conversation, the Nyah-Gwaheh growled angrily and reached under the trailer in pursuit of his quarry. Hayden, hidden from view by the spare tire casing and the toolbox, watched as the creature's long claws began to extend from the armored paw. Lilia, crawling on her stomach, backed as far as she could to the rear wheel. The claws got closer. Reaching up, Matt threw open the storage and drew out the truck's crow bar. Rolling under the chassis, he jabbed the wedge of the bar with all his might into the beast's paw. Recoiling in surprised pain, the Nyah-Gwaheh stood to his full twenty feet and let out a horrific roar.

"Now," said one of the miners. Taking their chances, the two sprang from their hiding placed under the trailer and made a dash into the clear, heading for the dump trucks. The angry bear roared again and fell across the trailer and its load to reach for the escaping prey. With one terrific backhand stroke of his forepaw, the Nyah-Gwaheh swiped at the men, sending them both into the air to smash against the mining equipment.

At the same time, Lilia screamed as the trailer bowed under the creature's full weight, nearly crushing her. Looking up, the Nyah-Gwaheh backed awkwardly from the trailer to give his attention to the two potential victims underneath. With his forefeet on the loaded trailer bed, he stood upright, leaned over, and reached under the trailer, catching a glimpse of the elusive targets. Snarling viciously, the creature thrust a deadly paw at Matt, who barely dodged the grasping claws while desperately looking around for anything that he could use to defend himself.

Suddenly, his eyes fell on the center latchet lock under the trailer—the single restraint holding all the steel rails onto the flatbed. Crawling madly for it, he evaded the creature's grasp, but only momentarily. With another frustrated effort, the angry beast wrapped his claws around him just as he reached the lock. Stretching out, Hayden clutched the mechanism and yanked on the release lever.

Matt turned his head away as the chain flew loose, whipping the Nyah-Gwaheh in the face. With a painful outcry, the creature dropped Hayden to the ground. An instant later, the steel rail load of the flatbed tumbled from the opposite side onto the beast's unprotected feet.

Matt and Lilia bolted for the sanctuary of the rocks as the creature roared in agony, clawing at the trailer and hauling it angrily over on its side.

Not far away, Webb and the men with him also took advantage of the distraction—darting toward the dump trucks in the hope of escape.

Webb himself leaped behind the wheel of the first truck, twisted the ignition, and rammed it into gear. Several of the miners leaped in or climbed into the truck bed as Webb gunned the engine and tore away, unmindful of any that hadn't been fast enough to scramble aboard. He was already fifty feet away when Ford arrived and scrambled into the remaining truck. Like Webb, Ford started the vehicle and, grinding the engine, began to pull away, unconcerned if anyone else escaped with him. Simmons climbed into the cab and other miners clambered into the back.

All of this commotion alerted the attention of the temporarily bruised monster. Pulling his feet free of the ponderous freight of the overturned flatbed, he crawled over the wreckage and quickly burst into a ferocious run in pursuit of the new prey. The second truck had not yet shifted into fourth gear when the charging beast leaped into the air and, extending his forepaws, landed heavily on the open-box bed, tumbling to his side. As the truck lurched from the bear's grasp, he angrily stood and bounded to the truck again. This time he lifted the truck off its rear wheels and thrusts it in rage to the ground. The truck continued to limp forward, but was obviously disabled, and the Nyah-Gwaheh pounced on the bed for the third time.

"The rear axle's busted," shouted Ford as he jumped from the truck, turning to face the full anger of the monster. He froze in terror while the creature stared down at him and roared, just as the other two miners tumbled from the open-box bed into the beast's path.

Backing away from the truck, Ford turned and broke into a sprint as the Nyah-Gwaheh fell on the other men in brutal fury.

Now only a frantic Simmons was left in the truck. Dragging himself into the driver's seat, he grabbed the gearshift, ground the truck into first, and shoved the gas pedal to the floor. The crippled vehicle only pitched helplessly a few feet as a huge shadow stole across the hood. Simmons began to whimper hysterically as he twisted to look out the open window. There, towering over the truck, stood the Nyah-Gwaheh. Roaring savagely, he reared up and fell with all his crushing weight upon the cab, again and again. Then, standing on his hind legs, the creature rent the air in a roar of final triumph, before surging away at top speed in the direction of the escaped vehicle.

Chapter 13

BATTLE AT THE MINING CAMP

Matt and Lilia ran from their place of refuge to the boulders by the canyon wall where Schindler, Thatcher and others had hidden for protection. The latter came out of their hiding place to meet them.

Schindler rushed to Lilia and embraced her. "Lilia! Matt! You frightened me to death. I'm so glad you're safe."

"Nobody's safe, Professor," said Hayden soberly as the rest of the company and additional ranchers surrounded them. "We've got to get our horses down from the bluff and go after that thing."

Tom was the first to speak. "I'm with you Hayden."

"I'm not!" said Buck, who was sitting on a rock nearby. His chest was wrapped in bandages, but the blood had still seeped through at five points. "You'll excuse me," he winced with obvious pain. "I think I have to bow out on this one."

Others of the ranchers began to express similar reluctance. "I'm afraid I agree with Buck, Matt," apologized Thatcher. "That thing is just too much for us."

"On the contrary," interrupted Schindler. "Up in the cave, we were at his mercy. The odds were all against us. But he's in our environment now. All the elements are to our advantage."

Matt held up his tranquilizing rifle. "If we use the tools at our disposal," he added. "But we have to work together and we'll have to work fast. If that thing gets beyond the reservation, there's no telling the damage it could do."

Hayden was suddenly distracted by something beyond the circle of the hunting party. Without explanation he walked resolutely through the small group. Glancing at each other they all followed him.

Surveying the destruction of the mining equipment, the miners were also arguing whether or not to follow the beast. Most were decidedly unenthusiastic. "What do you say, Ford?" one miner asked him.

The big man was hesitant. "Well," he stammered, "if enough of us go . . ."

His words were cut short as Matt Hayden stepped into the group. Holding the large-barreled rifle he stepped up to the foreman. "Ford, you've got something that belongs to me."

Ford looked at the rifle and recognized it. Backed up by the other miners, he straightened his frame and grinned in arrogance. "I could say the same thing to you. I found that rifle this morning. And you know what they say—'finders keepers.' I happen to know it's empty. So, hand it over." The foreman glanced around at his men who began to surround Hayden.

Their movement toward him was interrupted by the audible cocking of several guns. Stopping, they looked off to their side where the ranchers and braves stood with their guns drawn and pointed at them. "Now fellers," drawled Thatcher, "why don't we let these two boys handle this disagreement themselves."

Not waiting for any formalities, Ford threw the first punch, hitting Matt squarely in the face. Caught off guard, Matt struggled up and blinked as Ford advanced on him again, encouraged by the cheers of his men. Stepping into his stance, the foreman jabbed another powerful cuff at Hayden's face. But this time Matt jerked backward. Ford missed but was quick, instantly moving forward again with a roundhouse swing that was intended to end the fistfight with one blow. Matt ducked, and with Ford following through and off balance, the hunter landed a solid punch into Ford's abdomen. The big man wheeled around, swinging in pain, but not before Matt threw one fist, and then another into Ford's unguarded stomach. Ford doubled over slightly as Hayden came up with all the energy he had left, smashing the foreman in the jaw and sending him back into the midst of his subdued cheering section.

Ford lay still on the desert sand, flat on his back as Hayden stepped haltingly into the circle of men who now stood silent around Ford. Straddling over his vanquished foe, Matt reached down, fumbled in the pocket of Ford's loose jacket, and retrieved four nasty looking bullets as long as his hand, each with a rubber tip extending to a piercingly sharp point. Straightening, he smiled as he looked around at the stunned miners and slipped the tranquilizer bullets into his shirt pocket. "Finders keepers," he said, and he walked away to join his friends and the horses that were now waiting for them.

Webb was perspiring freely as he drove the dump truck along the dusty road from the canyon to Mammoth Steel's established mining area, a few miles to the west. The two men with him in the cab were silent. The four miners who had crawled into the open-box bed of the truck were anxiously looking at the road behind them, mindful that they were being pursued, though they could not see their pursuer.

"Give me that handheld," barked Webb, and one of his men passed him the handset from the radio transceiver. He twisted the knob on the dash and pressed the button on the device. "This is Webb. Are you there?" He waited a long moment.

"Yes, Mr. Webb," came a scratchy voice over the cab speaker. "What do you need?"

"I'll be to camp in about five minutes," he said. "I need you to put the entire area on alert."

"On alert?" the voice responded. "What's going on?"

"We're about to be attacked," Webb answered crossly. "Shut down operations. I want every man armed and every weapon we have readied for a fight."

"What . . . what is it?" stuttered the nervous operator, his voice more distorted now. "Is it the Japanese?"

"Shut up and just do what I say," shouted Webb into the handset. "It's worse."

A few minutes later, Jeremy Webb drove past the huge "Mammoth Steel Company" sign, which designated the nerve center of the company's mining operations. Known as "the camp," the area had grown from a simple blight of mining works to a huge terraced open pit a quarter of a mile across that scarred the once untouched beauty of the Garden of the Gods. Laced with rails, the open mine was a beehive of activity, buzzing with locomotives that hauled trains of mining cars to the surface at the edge of the gaping hole. Surrounded by operating conveyors, working steam shovels, and other active excavating equipment, the entire area hummed with the low, droning churn of machinery designed to plunder the earth of its resources and leave it defaced beyond recognition.

Webb sped into the compound and skidded to a stop as he and his men leaped from the truck. Perhaps twenty men were at the front gate waiting for him, while others stood in confused anticipation nearby. Much of the mine was still working. A manager appeared from a blockhouse and approached the arriving truck. The men followed him. Web stormed up to him angrily.

"Now, what's this about, Mr. Webb?" he asked.

""Shut up!" Webb screamed. "I told you to shut down and have every man ready, idiot." He turned to the men who came with him and to the employees at the gate. "Make a defensive line. Hurry! If you've got a weapon, make sure it's loaded. You're going to need it."

"I distributed all the guns we have, Mr. Webb," the manager defended. "Is it the Indians? If there's trouble, can't we call the sheriff?"

Webb turned to him, wide-eyed with fear. "Not against this."

In that instant a huge angry roar boomed forth from the hills surrounding the mining camp. At the sound, many of the men who had been curiously waiting backed away and ran. "Come back," Webb shouted.

"They have no weapons, Mr. Webb," yelled the manager.

Webb turned to those who remained. "Then those of you who do, take cover!" he bellowed. "And fight for your lives!"

Another roar tore the air. Instantly the camp became a bedlam of chaos. Miners at work left their stations in confusion. The entire pit began to look like a kicked anthill.

Miners from the truck took positions behind shacks of corrugated tin to ambush the creature. Webb ran along the tracks up an incline and hid with his rifle behind an idling steam shovel. Two men clambered up a set of steps to an isolated explosives shed while three others mounted one of the overhead works of several test shafts that dotted the flat area at the top of the huge pit. Others who had been provided with weapons took their places as best they could, anticipating the attack. None of them had long to wait.

Rounding the hillside entrance to the camp, the Nyah-Gwaheh appeared and stopped to survey the fence, the pit beyond it, and the myriad mechanical activities taking place as far as the eye could see. The creature stared, enthralled, viewing the entire panorama with a primitive awe. Cautiously proceeding, he lumbered through the huge gate portal and past the blockhouse to the edge of the terraced open pit. Slowly walking along the brink, he peered down the stepped slope, studying the motion of the ore conveyors, crushing machinery, and other mining apparatus. As he observed, he inadvertently bumped an empty ore car—stopping to watch as it rolled smoothly down the track. Fascinated, he turned and followed the car until it came to a halt. Then reaching out, he gave it a gentle shove before stopping it again on the track. Giving a loud snort, he began to playfully roll the car back and forth.

Throughout the beast's explorations, an eerie quiet permeated the entrance area, punctuated by the sounds of abandoned machinery pulsating across the expanse of the open pit. The men in positions of readiness waited anxiously for a signal from Webb to attack the monster.

Webb himself waited with eager anticipation in his place behind the vacated steam shovel. He watched as the beast, momentarily diverted from its rampage, leaned over the small gauge track to toy with the ore car. Glancing up at the extended arm of the idling shovel, Webb climbed up into the cab, released the brake, and hurriedly jumped to the ground. Slowly the shovel began to roll down the railed incline, gradually picking up speed as it headed toward the creature.

Webb looked to his miners with a signal of readiness, while the Nyah-Gwaheh, wholly distracted from them, continued to amuse himself with the mining car. Suddenly the accelerating steam shovel plummeted into the side of the unsuspecting beast. Tumbling to the ground before the weight of the crushing juggernaut, he grunted in surprise. At almost the same instant the boom crane, loosened by the collision, toppled down pinning him to the track.

"Now!" shouted Webb, leaping from his hiding place.

From every side, the miners began to open fire at the trapped creature. Men in positions level with the beast surrounded him on three sides, while men on the overhead works of the test shaft had a perfect vantage point to shoot down on him. And when he stood, men poised behind trucks on the terraced bench below him were prepared to attack him from a low angle. Wincing from this withering show of gunfire, the Naya-Gwaheh twisted himself from beneath the cumbersome crane of the steam shovel and angrily wrenched the scoop arm from the boom.

Feeling the bullets from the shooters on the level below him, the beast heaved the shovel cab off the tracks and down onto the terrace—sending miners and trucks tumbling over the crest of the bench into the pit.

Still enduring the bombardment from the overhead works of the mine shaft, the creature charged at the men on the tower. Within its latticework, two of the miners avoided his efforts to tear at them, while the other slipped into the cage of the vertical shaft for protection. Unable to reach the men in their stronghold, the frustrated beast began to twist the tower back and forth, finally snapping it off at its base. The overhead works toppled to the ground and into the open pit while the final man in the cage plummeted, screaming, down the mine shaft to his death.

As the creature roared into the exposed shaft, the gunfire renewed—and dynamite suddenly began to explode around him, hurled by the men at the explosives shack. Jeremy Webb stood at the entrance to the shack, dragging crates of dynamite within reach of his men. Stopping, he grabbed several of the sticks, wrapped a wire around them, and prepared to light his bomb.

Meanwhile, the monster flinched against the spray of bullets and explosions, retreating again to the edge of the pit and stumbling over the remains of the dismantled steam shovel. Shielding himself in anger, he grabbed the boom from the crane, flinging it in the direction of the dynamite shack.

Webb leaped from the shack to the level ground fifteen feet below as the scoop smashed through the walls of corrugated tin. The hut instantly burst into a ball of fire, showering the entire area with burning debris and shattered scrap metal amidst a thick haze of acrid smoke.

Coughing men vacated their places of concealment and staggered into the open area to evade the smoke and fill their lungs with breathable air. Hacking, they still held their rifles in readiness. But as the cloud of fumes cleared, the creature was gone. In the wake of the chaos of gunshots and dynamite blasts, there was relative quiet, interrupted only by the crackle of burning lumber and the scattered moans of men.

Suddenly, a huge roar ripped through the clearing smoke as the Nyah-Gwaheh leaped upon them, seemingly from nowhere. Men dispersed in full retreat as the creature gnashed its teeth and swept its bared claws at its prey, pursuing them down the sloping access road of the open mine. Everywhere across the quarter-mile expanse of the gaping pit tiny figures of men scattered in pandemonium before the brute force of a new master. Vanquished in battle, the defending miners at the entrance fled for refuge to a man-made plateau and waited as a quiet tension suddenly hung in the air. Trapped on that table of earth, a dozen men watched in horror as the creature blocked their only escape, surveyed them, and crouched for his attack.

At that moment, the sound of horse's hooves broke the relative silence and gunshots rang through the air. Fifteen ranchers on horseback galloped down the access ramp. Turning, the beast backed warily away from this new potential peril, while the cornered miners scrambled around him or down the sides of the broad plateau.

Meanwhile, the ranchers encircled the creature as if it were a raging bull at a rodeo. And, but for the size and ferocity of their target, the strategy they employed to bring down this beast was one they had all employed countless times in the arena or in the wild. At last, in this long day of struggle, the party of ranchers had the advantage in numbers, speed, and mobility. No longer trapped in the confines of a stifling cave, they were out in the open, armed with familiar tools and the skills to wield them. They were cowboys—and in this lopsided contest between man and beast, the odds were finally in their favor.

Still, the capture of the Nyah-Gwaheh was going to be desperate. None of them had ever ridden in a rodeo like this one. Having positioned themselves surrounding the creature, the moment of truth arrived as the ranchers took their lassos in hand.

Thatcher took the coiled rope at his saddle and loosened it as he turned to Schindler, who had also arrived on horseback. "Joe," he shouted, "you'd better rein in and watch this from the sidelines." Then he grinned. "This is the work of professionals."

As they rode around the confused creature, preparing their assault, a lone figure crawled to the edge of the bench just above the plateau. Blackened and bleeding from a gash in his forehead, Jeremy Webb crept to the crest of the terrace and smiled as he held up the several bundled sticks of dynamite. Poising himself to throw the destructive package, he struck a match to light the fuse. Suddenly the ricochet of a gunshot rang out at his feet. He shuddered and dropped the match as he looked up.

Lilia stood, twenty feet away, with a rifle trained on him. "Freeze, right where you stand, Mr. Webb!" she said calmly. "Because if you move a muscle, I swear, law or no law, I'll kill you—and I'll enjoy it."

Dropping the dynamite, Web stood like a statue in submission.

On the plateau below, the ranchers had surrounded the bear and were awaiting the signal from Hayden to lasso it. He didn't hesitate. "Now!" he cried, and a dozen loops of rope arched through the air to land and tighten around the neck and legs of the unsuspecting creature. Taken by surprise, he furiously shook off a few of the tethers. But others instantly flew at the beast, tangling him in a knot of cotton and nylon cables, which pulled at his massive legs and neck.

As the Nyah-Gwaheh roared in fury, the horses neighed and reared up with instinctive fear in the presence of a natural predator. Only the horses' trust in their riders restrained them from fleeing in terror.

Still, the brute strength of the beast made it obvious that the cowboys could not hope to subdue the creature with rope, or even restrain it for long. The plan was simple and well understood: hold the Nyah-Gwaheh long enough for Hayden to get a good shot with his tranquilizer rifle.

Atop his horse, and amidst the confusion, Matt was waiting for the bear to rear up to get a clear shot at his underbelly. Probably the most vulnerable portion of the creature's thick hide, the exposed abdomen offered the best, if not the only, hope of putting him to sleep. Suddenly, with one livid roar, the beast sprang up on his hind legs, clawing at the air and slashing at the ropes. Hayden took aim and pulled the trigger, just as one of the monster's massive talons sliced into several of the cords that held him in place. The result was instantaneous. Twisting, the Nyah-Gwaheh jerked to one side as the shot echoed through the open mine. The first of Hayden's precious rounds whizzed past the furious beast, plummeting into the wall of the pit.

Partially free, the animal lurched forward, angrily swinging for blood. Only ten lassos anchored to the horn of the rider's saddles now restrained the beast, who advanced in fury toward Matt. His panicked mare wheeled, faltered, and collapsed to her side. Hayden tumbled to the ground beside her as his big gun clattered onto the rocky soil several feet away. Getting to her feet, the horse galloped from the predator in wide-eyed terror, leaving Matt alone and unarmed in the path of the advancing beast.

"Matt!" Schindler ran into the "arena" on foot. Snatching up the treasured rifle, he tossed it to Hayden through the clouds of dust. No sooner had he done so than the back of the monster's paw struck the professor full force, propelling him twenty feet to the wall of the pit.

Other lassos were instantly flung around the creature's neck and limbs, but this time he tore loose of them as if they were made of thread and charged straight for Matt. Backpedaling, the hunter took aim again and tripped at the edge of the clearing. Falling on his back, he looked up to see the creature towering over him, poised for the kill. Jerking the rifle upright, he pulled the trigger. The recoil from the gun crushed his shoulder into the dust of the plateau as the remaining bullet shot from the gun's barrel and pierced the armored abdomen of the beast.

Standing on its hind legs, the Nyah-Gwaheh reeled in pain and staggered back. The men on horseback dropped their lines and galloped from his path to avoid being stuck by his flailing forepaws. Dazed and disoriented, the beast squinted around in every direction, settling onto all fours again. Deep in his chest a low growl began to build as he struggled to stay upright, tottering to one side and then to the other.

Hayden was now alone on the plateau. He lay on the ground, remaining absolutely still as the spell of the tranquilizer took effect. The eyes of the beast grew heavy and began to shut as he stumbled forward. Then those eyes squinted ahead, focusing on Matt. The beast opened his jaws into a fierce snarl and then he roared, filling the pit with terror from one end to the other as he stood erect and stepped unsteadily toward his final assailant. Suddenly the beast's legs collapsed beneath him as he fell forward. Matt rolled from the path of the lengthening shadow, just as the unconscious monster toppled beside him and tumbled over the edge to the terrace below.

Chapter 14

THE ABDUCTION OF GOD

Mike Thatcher was trying to wrap a bandage around Schindler's right arm as he lay prostrate on the couch in the great room of the ranch house. The professor also had his head heavily bound and wore a cast on his left arm. A crutch leaned at a broad angle against the couch. But in spite of his injuries, he was still very animated as he made an angry protest to a sheriff, who stood at the foot of the couch. "You can't do it!" the professor shouted angrily.

"Joe," Thatcher tried to constrain him, "the doctor said you're broken and bruised, inside and out. Now, will you hold still?"

Schindler jerked his arm away from the rancher and struggled painfully up on one arm. "I'm not going to hold still or stand still in the face of this travesty." Throwing the blanket from his legs he insisted on standing.

"Please, Joe," Thatcher pleaded. But he had no other choice but to help the professor to his feet.

Schindler, supported by his crutch, hobbled up to the sheriff. "You just can't do this and neither can they. The mining company has no right . . ."

"Mr. Schindler," the sheriff interrupted, "I've got nothing to do with it. It's the law now. And under declared martial law, Webb can do anything he pleases."

"And you're going to let him?" challenged Thatcher.

"I've got no choice, Mike," the sheriff answered. "With Simmons in his pocket, Webb controlled the reservation. Now, with Simmons out of the way, Webb pretty much owns it, at least for the time being. And he owns that prehistoric bear of yours too."

"So," Schindler countered angrily, "just like that, Mammoth Steel can hijack one of the greatest discoveries in the history of natural science." Wincing in pain, the professor stepped back as Thatcher helped him sit down again on the couch.

The sheriff stood helplessly. "Look," he said sympathetically, "you can take him to court. Get an injunction if you want."

"Right," spat Thatcher.

Hayden had been leaning against a wall nearby. "What's the point," he said bitterly, breaking his silence. "They're pulling out on the train tonight. Lilia told me by the time we can get any action from a court of jurisdiction, the Nyah-Gwaheh will already be stuffed and on display at the Smithsonian."

The sheriff glanced in Hayden's direction, gesturing to the huge stuffed grizzly that dominated the great room. "So," he reasoned, "in that sense, what is the difference between your big bear and this animal?"

Hayden didn't answer. He looked over his shoulder at the sheriff with a disgusted smirk and walked out the front door of the great room for some fresh afternoon air.

The sheriff looked back to Schindler. "I'm sorry I can't help you." Backing away, he began to leave, but then stopped and turned with an afterthought. "What the heck," he shrugged. "It's all for science anyway." Tipping his hat, he followed after Hayden. The sound of his footsteps on the hardwood floor faded away as the large door closed behind him.

Suddenly all was quiet in the great room as Schindler stared blankly ahead of him, overwhelmed with futility. Thatcher sat in a wicker chair and exhaled deeply as he rubbed his forehead. He glanced at his old friend and smiled. But it was Schindler who spoke first.

"What have I done to these people, Mike?"

"You can't blame yourself for this, Joe," Thatcher tried to console him. "Nobody's been a better friend to the Tonowa than you."

"Friendship!" Schindler repeated the word. It rang hollow in the air. "You know as well as I do, Mike, that my friendship to the Tonowa got lost in a blind ambition to establish the existence of the Nyah-Gwaheh."

"Nobody could have seen that coming," reasoned Thatcher. "Mammoth Steel was going to crush the Tonowa for the sake of profit no matter what happened. Nothing was going to change that. Your motives were different. You set out to prove a theory. Ironically, for better or worse, Jeremy Webb has helped you do it. Either way you look at it, you've been vindicated. You've got your reputation back. And science marches forward."

"At what cost," argued Schindler. "To the paleontological community, the Nyah-Gwaheh will be hailed as a monumental addition to the developmental timeline. And ten years from now it will all be forgotten in the wake of ongoing discoveries—a mere footnote in the textbooks of evolution. But when the Tonowa lose the Nyah-Gwaheh, there will pass from this earth a piece of sacred culture a thousand years old—and it will be gone forever."

"Up until today," he continued, "that creature was nothing more to me than a prehistoric trophy. But to these people, the Nyah-Gwaheh was their god. The faith of the Tonowa has become a needless casualty of the march of science."

"I wonder," mused Thatcher with a smile. "If the past one hundred years couldn't beat the faith out of the Tonowa, I'd be surprised if science can."

Schindler was inconsolable as he shook his head. "Still, I feel like I've betrayed them, Mike. I wish we could open that sealed cave—open it and bury everything we've learned from it deep inside that mountain where it belongs."

The sheriff caught up with Matt outside on the porch. "Oh, Mr. Hayden," he said in slight embarrassment. "I have orders to confiscate that big cage of yours." He gestured to the huge walls of an unassembled cage leaning against the house, just off the verandah.

"Eminent domain. I'm empowered by Mammoth Steel to pay you fifty dollars for it."

Hayden slowly smiled. "Great! It's worth five hundred." Reaching into his shirt pocket he handed the sheriff its contents with resignation. "Here's the key." The sheriff nodded but Hayden stopped him before he stepped away. "But if the Nyah-Gwaheh wants to get out of that cage, he won't need a key. I hope they realize what they have there."

The sheriff closed his fingers around the key thoughtfully and then turned and walked away. Hayden watched him go without another word.

Matt had stood for a long time at the gate of the main corral, watching the desert sunset. In his hand he held the strange yellow rock he'd picked up in the cave earlier in the day. Amber colored and speckled with gray and white, it was an unremarkable stone, like so much in the landscape that surrounded him. He looked around again at the broad expanse of the Vega Towachi: desert, rocks, blistering heat—and Indians. All of it was part of a beauty that was spectacular in the afternoon light of the setting sun. Unremarkable and yet dazzling, there was more to this people and to this land than met the eye. These mountains, canyons, and bluffs held secrets. And the natives here were the protectors of those secrets. They were a quiet, enigmatic people whose heritage allotted them the privilege to guard and defend something sacred and unknown. Now he knew it. The Garden of the Gods was a paradise that could not be seen with the naked eye. Its treasures were riches and beauties of the heart and soul. Perhaps that is what the Old Ones lost. And yet, now it was to be lost again, this time forever. He stared at the stone in his hand—the stone that was somehow the key to everything.

"A memento to mark th occasion?" Lilia's voice broke his concentration as she came up behind him. "A little something to remember the Indians by," she continued caustically. "A souvenir of Vega

Towachi and the Tonowa people—guardians of the Canyon de Dios and the cliffs of Oscura Mesa?"

Ignoring her sarcasm, Matt turned to her. "Lilia, what do you know about this stuff?"

The Indian girl took a casual glance at the rock and forced a bitter smile across her lips as she looked at Hayden. "The Tonowa creatively call it 'yellow rock.' The canyon is filled with it. Not much of a keepsake though. Now, if you really want a relic to show the folks back home, don't leave the reservation without this little prize."

Lifting her hand from her side she held out the pouch her grandfather had given her just the night before—the moment he died.

"This," she lamented bitterly, "is the sum total of one man's legacy. My grandfather was the descendant of a royal line a thousand years long. And yet after a hundred years of civilizing influence, this is all the modern world left him. The white men have stolen everything we ever had. One by one they robbed us of our land, our homes, our heritage, and our pride. I thought they'd taken everything they could. But I was wrong. Now, they've even taken our god."

Hayden's features hardened as he clenched the yellow rock in his hand. Dropping the stone, he turned to Lilia with determination, grabbing her by the shoulders. "Lilia!" he spoke firmly. "Listen to me. I can't take away the pain or the loss of the past hundred years. I can't even deal with my own heartache today. I've never felt more cynical in my life. We've all been robbed, do you understand? We've all lost something precious, even if it's nothing more than innocence, or hope—or faith, if that's what you want to call it."

Shaking her, he looked deeply into her face as her eyes filled with astonished tears. "The Hawate tried to teach me something yesterday—something about goodness and truth. Well, I don't know if I have a pure heart, but I know I can't walk away today without trying to prove to myself that I do. Some things can be snatched away from us by evil and godless men. And we may have lost those things. But some things can never be taken away. Things in here," Matt touched his hand to his chest. "Stone Bear knew it. And so do those homeless Tonowa living out under the stars. They know it. To them it's all wrapped up in their god, whether he was in that cave or not."

"But the Nyah-Gwaheh's gone, Matt," whispered Lilia as the tears rolled down her face. "And Webb didn't just take him. We practically gave him away."

"Maybe, Lilia," he said and then paused. "But I intend to bring him back. Still, to do the impossible I'm going to need help. Lilia, cynics are a dime a dozen. A cynic cannot help me work a miracle. I need someone who believes in something." Matt held up the leather pouch and stared at her.

Without a word she looked intently into his eyes, and gently wiped the tears from her own. Taking the leather pouch from him, she nodded with silent resolve.

Hayden creased his brow. The decision had been made. "Get hold of Tom Running Wolf and the other men of the tribe. Tell them to meet me here as quickly as possible." Stooping down, Matt picked up the mysterious yellow stone. "Meanwhile, I've got to talk to Schindler about this rock. But we've all got to hurry. There's not much time."

Chapter 15

RESURRECTION

The last bare hint of twilight was just fading from the sky as the train was being readied to leave the Towachi station. Miners milled busily and excitedly about, seeing that all was in order on the locomotive and the seven cars attached to it. The entire line consisted of a steam engine, a coal tender, a dining salon, four ore hoppers, and, at the end of the train, a flat car.

The flat car was the center of attention tonight as the train prepared to leave. Jim Ford stood on the wooden floorboards shouting orders at several men who were securing the joints of a large barred enclosure.

"Check the corners of that cage," Ford barked. "I don't want 'em to budge an inch."

"For cryin' out loud, Ford!" one of the men turned on the foreman. "It's a cage! It's gonna rattle a little. But it ain't comin' loose. We've double-reinforced every joint. And I've checked each one of 'em myself three times."

Ford grabbed the man by the shoulder and jerked him around. "I don't care how many times you've checked 'em," he shrieked. "Check 'em again."

"You seem a little uneasy, Ford." The foreman turned to see Webb on the ground leaning against the flat car. He looked up at Ford and smiled as he enjoyed a cigarette.

Ford walked over to him. "You bet I'm uneasy!" he grumbled. "I don't like this. I don't like it one bit."

153

Webb casually climbed the side access ladder and stood on the flat car. "Ford," he said calmly as he faced him, "you've been around the Indians too long. It's contaminated you. Made you superstitious—even delusional." He gestured inside the barred enclosure mounted firmly on the center of the flat car. "Look at him."

Ford shifted his eyes to look at the Nyah-Gwaheh. The fearsome animal was sedated, chained, and encased in an impregnable cage with one-inch-thick steel bars. "Why he's got enough tranquilizer pumped into him to knock him out for days. He's chained to the flatcar so he couldn't move a muscle if he wanted to. And he's surrounded by four walls of steel."

Webb turned to look at Ford. "And just in case, we've got 30 men in the dining car armed with elephant guns. Now what more can you ask than that?"

But Ford was doggedly insistent—and afraid. "I just don't like it, that's all. You haven't been close to this thing. So close that you could feel its breath. You haven't touched that skin—like sandpaper. And you haven't looked it in the eye. There's anger and hatred and vengeance in those eyes. Vengeance, Webb." He looked back at the sleeping beast. "And he means to have it."

Webb coolly threw his cigarette to the ground, and then grabbed Ford violently by the lapels of his jacket. "Now you look me in the eye, Ford," he sneered. "I mean to have a few things too. Can you see it in my eye, Ford? And that thing in the cage isn't going to stop me."

Webb slowly relaxed his hold on Ford. Straightening out his collar, he continued amiably. "Now don't get sloppy on me, foreman. We're gonna be big heroes when we arrive in Houston with this thing. Meanwhile," he stepped to the cage, "you just think of our armor-skinned friend here as a great big overstuffed teddy bear."

With that, he reached through the cage with the butt of his rifle and gave the shoulder of the Nyah-Gwaheh a solid jab. Instantly the beast's forepaw pulled away in reaction. Both Webb and Ford aimed their guns, jumped back a step, and watched. The creature continued to sleep. Webb didn't look at Ford. "And tell the men if it so much as stirs, they are to kill it without hesitation."

"Yes, Mr. Webb," said Ford, whose eyes were also locked on the beast.

Webb turned and walked away soberly. Ford followed him as the train's bells and whistle signaled their departure. The locomotive and its seven-car burden slowly pulled from the depot. The final journey of the Nyah-Gwaheh was underway.

As the train gradually rolled from the Towachi whistle stop, a figure emerged from behind the tank of the small water tower and leaped through the waning twilight, landing on the coal tender. Rising up carefully in the darkness, Matt Hayden signaled to someone on the ground with a wave of his hand.

Below, hidden in the shadows of the trading post, Tom and a small group of braves watched. "Quickly." Tom turned to the other Indians, "we've got less than half an hour to get to the reservoir. Hayden's doing his part. Now let's do ours."

Among the dispersing miners, no one noticed the Indians as they stepped from the darkness and mounted their horses beside the trading post. Turning their ponies east, they rode purposefully off in the direction of the San Juan River.

Hayden stood cautiously and began to make his way to the flat car at the rear of the train. Letting himself down from the tender, he wiped off his hands and climbed the ladder to the roof of the dining car. Under his feet, he heard the voices of the miners assigned to guard duty. They were already in high spirits—eating and drinking as their adventure began. He walked gently across the roof, careful not to alert them of his presence. The high-profile dining car rocked under his feet as the locomotive picked up momentum and reached a comfortable speed for the canyons and passes of the desert terrain. The whistle blew again, signaling the confidence of the engineer and the passengers as the train plunged into the night.

Climbing down onto the first ore hopper, Hayden continued his awkward hike across the rubble, stumbling as he made his way over a pathway in constant motion. Moving across the four freight cars, Matt finally arrived at the flat car where the Nyah-Gwaheh was caged. He smiled at the thought of the placement of the beast on the last car of the train. He was sure that Webb and Ford wanted the monster as far from them as possible.

Stepping guardedly onto the flat car, he carefully approached the cage and looked at the creature. He had been this close before, but never with the quiet opportunity to consider him. "What are you, my friend?" he asked himself. "And what are you doing here?" He shook his head. This beast was a miracle. But beyond that reality, he had no idea what to make of him.

Snapping back to the real world, Hayden glanced quickly behind him and reached into his jacket. Retrieving a stiff wire from his pocket, he knelt beside the cage and began to work at the lock.

Miles away, at the rim of the dammed San Juan Reservoir, a more ambitious project was underway. A large group of Indians, both men and women, had gathered at the edge of the manmade lake. Working resolutely, and without speaking, the gathered tribes people were piling a huge load of wood, brigade fashion, atop the train tracks that ran by the dam.

As the Tonowa people labored at their task, a group of riders galloped over the rim of the reservoir, stopping to observe the work of their people in the moonlight. Looking around, Tom Running Wolf spotted Lilia, standing well apart from the group, before a small, flickering campfire. "Go and help them with the barricade," Tom told them. "I'll be right there."

The other braves cantered to the work in progress as Tom turned his pony and plodded over to Lilia. He found her deep in thought, staring into the trembling flames. Dismounting, he came up beside her. "Lilia," he said tentatively, "can you do this?"

The sound of labor continued to echo across the desert sand as Lilia slowly nodded without taking her eyes from the fire. "I am the granddaughter of Stone Bear—the Hawate. For many years he taught me the old ways. He prepared me for this. Now I owe it to him." She glanced off to the Indians laboring at the wooden barricade. "And we owe it to them."

Tom half smiled and then grew serious. "But they're the old ways, Lilia. How can we be expected to observe the rituals that we no longer believe?"

She turned her head to look at the skeptical brave and the hint of a smile passed over her lips. "Put out the fire, Tom," she said.

Tom stepped to the fire and extinguished the struggling yellow flames under his boots. As he did so, Lilia stood back and, with a long pointed rod in her hands, began to draw a large circle around the spot where the tiny fire had been. Tom watched as she circled the ashes once again, making an even larger circle in the sand. Stopping, she raised her hands into the air from her sides, holding them midway as a low note of a chant began to resonate deep in her chest, which grew until it burst from her open mouth.

Tom backed away from the blackened spot and stepped from the circle as he watched. Entranced by the ceremony, he gradually became aware of others surrounding the blackened center. Having finished the barricade, the Tonowa approached the sacred place in reverent silence and stood as wordless witnesses.

Without acknowledging the growing crowd of worshippers, Lilia stepped to the center of the circle and knelt on the ground. She carefully removed bits of tinder and kindling from her coat pocket and arranged them on the ground atop the ashes of the dead fire. She then set the pointed end of the rod in the center of the ashes and tinder and began to rotate it between the palms of her hands. Spinning the stick, she brought her hands down the length of it, to the bottom—once, twice, three times before she stopped, and put more dry tinder upon the powdery embers, blowing on it delicately until a spark flashed up and erupted into a tiny yellow flame. Lilia gently fed the fire with grass and small kindling until it blazed with a life of its own—a bright orange/red flame that illuminated those who looked into it with a rich glow of warmth.

Hayden continued struggling with the lock until he heard a soft click. Smiling, he dropped the wire and began to open the lock when he was suddenly interrupted by a voice behind him, shouting above the volume of the rattling train wheels and the belching of the locomotive.

"Well, well, well. What have we got here?"

Hayden slowly turned his head to see Webb, standing with Ford at the end of the flat car. Both of them had their rifles pointed at him.

"If it isn't the irrepressible Mr. Matt Hayden," continued Webb, "who keeps getting himself into mischief. It's just one thing after another. Of course, finding you here is certainly no surprise." Webb shook his head sarcastically. "But still disappointing, Hayden. Predictably disappointing. And when the authorities find your body by the railroad tracks with a bullet through your chest, they won't even ask questions at the inquest. Because this time, it's not just tres- passing or inciting to riot or even assault. This time it's theft—theft of federal property with malicious, murderous intent."

Webb smiled and nodded to the foreman. "Ford, do the honors." With grim satisfaction, Ford raised his rifle to fire.

"Tell me about theft," challenged Hayden, "or fraud, or even treason. Which will it be, Webb?" With that challenge, Matt slowly opened his hand. In his open palm he held the enigmatic yellow rock speckled with gray and white flecks.

Momentarily stunned, Ford lowered his rifle. But Webb remained unruffled.

"I found this rock in the cave this morning," Matt continued. "It matched the samples in some bags I also found on the cave floor. But it's not iron ore. This is what you're after, isn't it, Webb?"

Webb laughed out loud. "What would I want with that useless Indian yellow rock?

"Useless?" Hayden shouted above the rattle of the train. "Professor Schindler told me this afternoon that the Americans and the British are secretly working to develop a bomb." He held up the rock. "This is the stuff that makes it go."

The smile disappeared from Webb's face and he glanced at Ford. Hayden went on. "It's called uranium. It's very valuable. Only you're not planning on sending this uranium to Los Alamos or London. You're exporting to Berlin."

Webb's expression was now a dark shadow of hatred. Hayden forged ahead. "Every engineer or surveyor marks his sample points in the rock. Your engineers were no different. Only they marked their sample point with a swastika."

"Stupid idiots!" grumbled Ford.

"Shut up, Ford," barked Webb. "You haven't been too bright yourself." He focused on Matt. "You, on the other hand, Mr. Hayden, have figured everything out perfectly."

"Not until this minute," confirmed Matt. "It was all an educated guess until you verified it . . . just now."

Webb continued to glare at Hayden, until a mirthless grin creased the corners of his mouth. "Clever. So the hunt goes on. Yes as a matter of fact, this train—with that monster as our high-profile passport—is carrying the first shipment of low-grade uranium to Houston, where a Dutch freighter is waiting to deliver it to Germany. We'll be back though. The quality mineral is still in the canyon, embedded into the walls of that cave. And after all, Hayden, there is a war on."

Webb laughed again. The moment of concern had passed. What did he have to worry about from Matt Hayden or anyone else?

The bright orange flame danced in the breeze. Lilia sat before the fire. The other Indians sat outside the circle she had drawn in the sand. On her lap she had laid the pouch Stone Bear had given her just the night before. Opening it, she took its contents in her fingers and held them out before the flame in the light wind.

Many of the herbs in her hand she recognized: white sage, sweet grass, juniper bark, bear root, lavender flowers, and leaves of tobacco and corn. But others were unfamiliar to her: stalks of desert plants, seed pods, twigs of different trees, and various pollens wrapped in a tiny, folded envelope made of very old paper. One by one, she began to lay the items upon the small fire. As she did so, she chanted. "Shongo-rabi, Nyah-Gwaheh. Walta orapi pokan." Each token that Lilia placed upon the tiny fire gave birth to a new flame. Vibrant shades of orange, red, yellow, green, and blue burst forth from the sand as rich fragrances filled the air and touched the senses in a worship ceremony of quiet devotion, reverence, and peace.

"Kayendara Windago kaikut," intoned Lilia. "Tonowa tan sho-shonto."

Webb was full of self-assured confidence now. He was prepared to end this drama. Hayden knew something. And that something was far too much. So the solution was easy. Erasing Hayden had been part of Webb's solution from the beginning anyway. He lifted his rifle chest high, "Now, Hayden," he gestured with the gun, "move over here, away from that cage. We wouldn't want to risk disturbing that precious animal, no matter how sound asleep he appears to be."

Gradually, Hayden and his antagonists traded places on the flat car, until Webb and Ford had positioned themselves between the game hunter and the Nyah-Gwaheh. "That's far enough," shouted Webb. There was a long pause as he smiled.

"Well," Hayden raised his voice defiantly, "what are you waiting for?"

Webb lifted the gun to eye level, aiming point-blank at Matt. But still, he seemed to be waiting for something as he stared Hayden down.

Lilia had placed every talisman on the fire but one. She spoke the last of the words, which she had memorized from the Old Tongue.

"Mappa cascawa, Nyah-Gwaheh." With those syllables she placed the tiny folded envelope of faded paper onto the fire. It burst into flames of every hue with a crackle of sparks and a plume of smoke. As she did, a peal of thunder rolled across a cloudless sky.

A drumming of thunder clapped in the distance, blending with the grinding roll of the train's wheels on the tracks. And in that instant the Nyah-Gwaheh opened his eyes. Without a sound, the creature turned his head to look up at Webb and Ford, who were still waiting with their backs to the beast. Matt's own eyes grew in amazement and terror as he watched the monster's mouth curl into a noiseless snarl.

Webb smiled and lowered his rifle only slightly. "What am I waiting for, Hayden? That! I was waiting for dread to overcome that cool reassurance of yours."

As Webb spoke, Hayden continued to observe the Nyah-Gwaheh. Quietly, the beast pulled against the chain wrapped around one foreleg. Straining with his massive strength, the creature pulled the shackle taught. And then suddenly, the chain snapped. As the train bounced over the desert terrain, the two miners didn't distinguish the sound of the breaking fetter from the metallic clatter of the cage. Still the Nyah-Gwaheh made no abrupt movement, but shifted slowly within the enclosure.

Webb, oblivious to the drama behind him, laughed out loud. "If the National Geographic could only see the look on your face now." Shaking his head, he smirked with disgust. "Hunt 'em and Hold 'em Hayden! But this is one time you won't even be bringing yourself back alive."

Matt continued to watch as the Nyah-Gwaheh slowly reached out with both paws to the wall of the cage in front of him. The train whistle blew as the creature shoved his paw against the enclosure door, nudging it open several inches.

"Now," continued Webb, "let's make this look good. Take a few steps backward to the edge of the car." Hayden backed slowly away as

Webb advanced with his rifle. Ford lowered his weapon and watched with a cruel grin. Only a few feet separated the foreman from the cage, behind which the creature slowly stood on all fours and poised himself for the kill. And then, baring his teeth, the Nyah-Gwaheh thrust his paw through the space he'd opened in the cage door.

"Look out!" Hayden shouted in spite of himself. Instantly Ford spun on his heels and raised his rifle. But the foreman had scarcely turned when the monster sunk his extended claws deep into his chest. With a terrific roar, the Nyah-Gwaheh dragged Ford screaming, through the open door, into the cage.

Momentarily frozen, Webb watched in horror and listened as Ford's screams abruptly ended. Coming to himself, he jerked the rifle up to shoot when Hayden tackled him from behind. The rifle discharged into the air and clattered to the edge of the cage as Webb and Hayden tumbled to the floor of the flat car. And all the while the Nyah-Gwaheh fought furiously to tear himself from his shackles and from the cage.

Wrestling in a struggle of life and death, Hayden and Webb rolled to the edge of the flat car. Until now, Matt had not considered how this long and strenuous day had taxed his reserves. He was the exhausted underdog in a battle with an implacable enemy. But that enemy's focus was divided. Webb glanced quickly between the monster in the cage and the man clutched in his grip—torn by his terror of the creature on the one hand and his maniacal drive to murder his nemesis on the other. Madness filled Webb's features and his heart as he tightened his fingers around Hayden's throat and began to wrench the breath from his life. But another deafening roar from the beast and the metallic whine of the scraping cage walls tore the killer's attention away for a split second. Matt thrust his arms upward, knocking Webb's hands from his throat, and tumbled with him to the center of the car. As they fell apart, Webb rolled upright and leaped again at the prostrate hunter. Matt was prepared. Doubling up, he kicked out his legs, thrusting Webb across the flat car.

Sprawling next to the edge of the cage, Webb looked up in panic as the Nyah-Gwaheh glared down on him behind the bent and twisted bars. Suddenly, Webb also saw his rifle, lying at the base of the broken cage. Reaching for it, he grabbed the barrel end and yanked away, just ahead of the creatures grasping claw. The beast let out a frenzied snarl as his talons scratched five long, deep gouges in the wooden floor.

Crazed with rage, Webb turned and lunged at Hayden, swinging the butt end of the rifle at him. As he did so, the hunter ducked and the murderous swipe went askew, sending Webb off balance to the floor and over the side of the flat car. Hanging perilously by his fingers, he dangled over the fleeting terrain of a desert canyon, which gaped below him.

Matt stood like a statue, staring between Webb who clung precariously to the edge of the car, and the Nyah-Gwaheh, who fought in an insane fury to liberate himself from the steel manacles and the walls that entrapped him. He was almost free from the snare of chains and twisted bars. In a split-second decision, Hayden dove to the brink of the car and, reaching over the edge, pulled Webb back to safety.

The two of them rolled breathlessly to the surface of the car just as the beast broke free of his prison with an ear-splitting cry of emancipation. Without a moment's hesitation, they both scrambled away, off the flat car and up the end of the linking ore hopper with the creature in full pursuit.

Running atop the ore of the open car, they scrambled awkwardly over the uneven payload. Matt glanced back to see the Nyah-Gwaheh climbing from the flat car to the ore hopper. Looking around, the creature spotted them and bound forward with a low roar. Matt turned and jumped to the second car in an effort to catch up with Webb. But in his leap across the linkage gap to the third car, Matt's footing faltered on the uneven chunks of ore. Falling painfully onto the jagged rocks, he glanced up. Just ahead of him, Webb looked back and hurried on without breaking stride.

Matt knew he was in trouble. He rolled over quickly, scraping the skin of his hands on the sharp ore and squinting into the darkness. The beast was almost upon him. With no hope of escape, he continued to push himself, tumbling to the end of the car and into the gap between the two hoppers. Falling down the end ladder, Matt steadied himself and crouched by the linkage as the creature peered over the space and looked down on its cornered prey.

Reaching down between the cars, the Nyah-Gwaheh grasped at Hayden, who twisted from the path of its razor talons. The claws grated on the bare metal of the coupling and then came at him in another attempt. Again Matt barely dodged the clutches of the angry beast. But suddenly as he spun from the monster's grasp, he slipped on the narrow footing of the hopper's frame. In almost slow motion, he fell, jarring into the linkage, and then felt himself toppling, head first between the cars to the tracks below.

In that instant, the needle-pointed claws of the Nyah-Gwaheh pierced his left shoulder and sank deep into the muscles of his upper back and chest. He screamed in agony as the beast held him there, suspended inches above the speeding tracks, before lifting him slowly from certain death. Dragging Hayden up between the cars, the creature lifted him ruthlessly to the open air where he spread wide his claws and dropped the body of his limp captive onto the ore hopper. Delirious with pain, Matt opened his eyes languidly and looked almost blankly up into the night sky. In an instant the head of the beast filled his vision as he gaped open his jaws, filling the air with a deafening roar, which was carried away by the desert wind.

The cry faded away and a thick and pungent stench from the monster's breath filled Matt's nostrils. He lay there, in motionless agony and dread. Debilitated from the sting still pulsing from his shoulder, he hadn't the strength to move. Waiting powerlessly, he anticipated his final moment of life and closed his eyes again.

But the beast made no move to kill him. Opening his weary eyes, Matt looked again at the creature, who held him with a steady glare. His huge mouth curled into an open snarl. And then he began to sniff the air around him. After a few short intakes of breath, the monster snorted as he lifted his head to survey the night air. Stopping, he gazed toward the front of the train, took one last glance at Hayden, and then paced purposefully, relentlessly toward the dining car and the locomotive.

Chapter 16

REBIRTH

Webb jumped from the last ore hopper and paused breathlessly on the landing of the dining car. As he considered what to do next he heard a deep roar rumble through the night. Without hesitation, he climbed the ladder to the top of the car and scrambled across its roof. Stopping at the front end of the car, he crouched low and took another look back.

There, two cars back, he could just make out the hunched figure of the Nyah-Gwaheh lurching toward him. Webb glanced down at a small flue pouring a steady stream of kitchen smoke into the desert air, and hurriedly leaped to the relative safety of the coal tender. The pleasant odors of the exhaust, smoke, and grease from the miners' meal continued to emanate in the beast's direction, serving as a beacon to a god who was hungry for revenge.

Inside the dining car, thirty men sat lounging, eating, and otherwise enjoying themselves. Without warning, a huge claw crashed through the roof of the car and began to grope for the men inside. In pure pandemonium, the miners evaded one claw, while the other ripped at the hole in the roof. Two of the men dodged the fumbling paw, dashing to the rifle rack, just as the beast tore away a huge chunk of the roof. Jerking out an elephant gun each, they took desperate aim and fired.

The bullets hit their mark, slashing into the creature's shoulder. Reeling back in pain, he bellowed into the night, and then, unmindful of the wound, leaped back to the car in fury. By now, others had scrambled to the gun rack as the Nyah-Gwaheh swung his powerful foreleg at them. The angry swipe crushed the miners against the rack while crashing the wall to splinters that showered over the desert.

Enraged, the beast now clawed toward each man who remained trapped in the car. One by one he reached for them, and one by one he claimed an awful vengeance in their destruction. When the car was finally demolished and all the miners were dead, he lifted his head skyward and roared again in conquest. But his moment of victory was momentary. Looking up, he squinted through the smoke of the belching locomotive. Relentlessly, he crawled toward the coal tender and the engine, where Webb had hidden.

Beside the dam on the San Juan Reservoir, hundreds of Tonowa waited in the silence of the moonlit night. A huge barricade of wood now covered the railway tracks. And they stood—men, women, and children—many of them holding torches, anticipating in reverence and hope, the arrival of the train and its cargo. Suddenly, the mournful sound of a distant locomotive whistle broke the tense stillness. Tom Running Wolf broke from the group and ran to an elevation of rocks and peered into the darkness. Afar off, he recognized the figure of the approaching train as it wove its way through the desert coming toward them.

Leaping from the rocks, Tom hurried with his torch back to the barricade, looked at the expectant faces of his people, and applied his light to the kindling under the massive barrier. The flame burst skyward and grew with a life of its own until, within seconds, the woodpile erupted into a blazing wall of fire across the railroad tracks. Slowly the people backed away from the flame on both sides until only one figure was left before the fire.

Lilia stood by the light of the fire and bowed her head as if it were a holy altar. As the flames illuminated her face with a powerful radiance, she looked up, turned, and walked solemnly away.

On the train, Hayden heard the destruction of the dining car and the screams of men. Weakly he rolled onto his side and looked lethargically toward the front of the train. But suddenly his eyes grew wide as he caught sight of a brilliant yellow light far ahead on the gradually curving track. He squinted in the distance as the flaming barricade came into focus. Forcing himself to move in spite of his pain, he dragged his body to the rear of the hopper car and staggered weakly down the end ladder, where he crumpled into the space beneath the ore bin.

Matt took a deep breath and pulled himself upright. Clutching onto the support bars with his weakened left arm, he reached with his opposite hand under the linkage in search of the uncoupling rod—a desperate effort to detach the end cars from the rest of the train. Excruciating pain pulsed through his shoulder and back as he groped in the darkness for the elusive lever. Then, suddenly, he felt the crank-shaped shaft in his fingers, grabbed it with all the strength he had left, and wrenched it up and outward. With a loud metallic clink, the cars uncoupled, followed by the popping of the break line as the train ahead gradually pulled away and lengthened the distance between them. Matt collapsed limply beside the linkage as the two uncoupled cars reduced their speed and fell behind. Still, there was no escaping the pile-up that was now only moments away. The collision that was coming would require a miracle to survive.

Webb had been watching the Nyah-Gwaheh from the "high ground" of the coal tender, feeling hopeful and even confident that he had eluded death at the hands of this relentless foe. But then the monster peered up across the length of the coal car—almost directly at him— still intent on his pursuit of destruction. Webb shuddered and grit his teeth in frustration as he leaped down to the locomotive cab. The engineer, startled by his arrival, looked nervously between Webb, the tracks ahead, and the clamor taking place on his train "What are you doing? And what's going on back there?" he demanded.

"Just drive!" Webb shouted angrily. Looking about the cab, he spotted the engineer's rifle. Jerking it from its holster, Webb climbed back up the end of the coal tender, carefully staying as low as possible. From that vantage point he could see the dark figure of the creature, peering through the smoke, working its way toward the engine, and examining every recess for signs of an elusive prey. Satisfied, the beast moved relentlessly forward onto the coal car.

Standing from his hiding place, Webb took aim and shot the rifle, repeatedly. Surprised, the creature recoiled for an instant, then he lunged forward onto the coal tender in spite of Webb's defensive assault. Retreating to the locomotive cab, Webb continued to shoot, while the Nyah-Gwaheh charged toward him, fumbling through the torrent of bullets and the smoke of the locomotive.

Watching in horror, the terrified engineer took a quick glimpse at the tracks ahead and jolted with alarm. Five hundred feet away a huge barricade of fire blazed on the tracks, blocking the path of the train. Reaching quickly for the throttle, he instantly began to slow the locomotive.

Webb turned to him in an insane fury. "What are you doing?"

"See for yourself," shouted the engineer as he pointed ahead on the tracks. "We can't go through that. We'll derail."

Without pausing to argue, Webb grabbed the coal shovel from its hook on the tender and struck the engineer in the head. "Oh, yes we can," he growled as the engineer fell to the floor. Seizing the throttle, he gave the locomotive full steam.

The Indians on the periphery of the tracks had been watching the locomotive slow down. Suddenly the train burst into its maximum throttle, picking up speed. As it did so, the Tonowa on both sides of the tracks turned and scattered in panic as the train bore down on the barricade.

Jeremy Webb turned from the window and reached again for his rifle. But in that moment the Nyah-Gwaheh lunged through the smoke to the locomotive cab. Raising his gun to shoot, Webb instinctively backed away from the creature, into the seething boiler. He shrieked in pain and jerked away, just as the beast reached through the cab, driving his claws into Webb and pinning him against the boiler. The vice president of Mammoth Steel screamed in indescribable agony.

At that instant, the locomotive plowed full speed into the flaming barricade. Shards of burning wood flew into the air, showering from the sky for hundreds of feet as the train derailed in a deafening din of squealing machinery and grinding metal. Plunging into the sand, the steam locomotive exploded into a thousand pieces as the train of cars behind it upended, cast in every direction, and burst into flames. In several seconds the destruction settled into a wake of motionless chaos.

The smell and sounds of the burning wreckage filled the air, mingling with an acrid smoke as the Tonowa crept slowly from their retreats to witness the aftermath of the devastation. From a corner of the smoldering ruin, Hayden painfully emerged from the remains of the ore car, torn and bloodied, but alive. Struggling free of the crash debris, he collapsed to his knees on the sand and looked about him. Then his eyes fell on a scene that made his blood run cold. Standing unsteadily, he gazed upon it with a strange grief.

In the light of the flaming wreck, the lifeless body of the Nyah-Gwaheh lay in a crumpled heap on the desert sand. Matt's feet were planted in the ground. Unable to move for utter shock, he took in the picture, crestfallen.

He became aware of many others who stopped to stare in speechless angst at the tragedy. Tears would not have been enough. The loss of a cultural treasure lay on the ground, surrounded by the shadows of destruction. Illuminated by the dancing fires of the wreckage, Lilia and her people slowly gathered around the creature's body in a wide circle.

A short distance away Schindler, Thatcher, and Buck arrived in a pickup truck and stopped. Sweeping over the collision site, they found Hayden and approached him sullenly. No words were spoken as they stood beside him and sadly looked on.

Still, the Tonowa remained in mourning. In the flickering light of the burning wreck they stood silently, worshipfully as they looked upon the remains of the beast.

Then, suddenly, almost unperceptively at first, one of the claws of the creature moved. Startled, Tom Running Wolf backed away. A few others also retreated a step. But most of the hundreds of worshipers remained, committed, in place. Lilia touched Tom's arm and gently pulled him back into the circle. "No, Tom," she said. "Don't be afraid."

Slowly and ever so slightly, the Nyah-Gwaheh continued to move with signs of life as the Tonowa people watched on. Laying on his side, he pushed himself prostrate and began to drag his crushed and bleeding body over the sand. As he did, the Indians made way before him, moving with him, all the while continuing to encircle him without fear.

In obvious pain, the beast struggled agonizingly from the ground onto all fours and finally forced himself upright, rising in strength to his hind legs. Illuminated in the firelight, the Nyah-Gwaheh looked around and roared defiantly as the Tonowa people continued to gaze up at him with devout reverence. Even Schindler, Thatcher, Hayden, and Buck came near, staring up at the creature in awe.

Taking a final look at his worshipers, the creature turned from them, fell to all fours and limped painfully to the edge of the reservoir through a gap that the people had opened for him. Stopping at the wall of the dam, the Nyah-Gwaheh gave one last terrible roar that filled the night and then, leaning over the dam, plunged himself head first into the waters below.

Gradually, all who witnessed the scene gathered at the edge of the dam to look, many with tears in their eyes, down into the black water as the ripples settled on the surface. The Nyah-Gwaheh was gone.

As their faces continued to glow in the scattered firelight, Professor Schindler spoke quietly. "There are hundreds of fissures and caverns in this canyon—crevices in the volcanic rock that he has known for a thousand years. He's gone to find one of them, to crawl deep into the bowels of the earth, and to rest."

Coming to stand beside Matt, Lilia looked up at him with a peaceful expression. Schindler continued. "And there he'll wait perhaps another hundred years for his time to come—when his people call upon him."

"Then," whispered Lilia, "let us leave him there to sleep—protected and undisturbed." Turning to those who had assembled on the edge of the dam, she spoke in a quiet tone, but one that all could hear. "My friends, what we have seen, and what we have felt, we must cherish in our hearts. But this knowledge can never leave the Vega Towachi." The light of a thousand fires burning on the desert sand illuminated her face. "The secret of the Nyah-Gwaheh must remain forever hidden in the Garden of the Gods."

Chapter 17

EXALTATION

FROM AN ARTICLE PRINTED IN THE
AMERICAN GEOGRAPHIC MAGAZINE, 1958.

There is, on the northeastern corner of Arizona, a vast stretch of desert known as the Vega Towachi. Spilling into the bordering states of Utah, Colorado, and New Mexico, the thousand-square-mile expanse of land makes up the most forbidding portion of the Navajo reservation and was once referred to by the ancestors of those people as "The Garden of the Gods."

A peculiar wrinkle in history surrounds a tiny spot on the Vega Towachi just north of the Indian trading post/train depot of the greater Tonowa Reservation in northwestern Arizona. Identified on the map as Oscura Mesa, these volcanic mountains are home to the remnants of the nearly extinct Tonowa Indian nation. Living in a small network of cliff dwellings in a valley called by them the "Canyon de Dios," the Tonowa consider their homeland sacred—a dispensation of the gods. And out of respect to the Tonowa and their religion, the larger Navajo nation has, for hundreds of years, relinquished to that tiny tribe all rights of occupancy regarding Oscura Mesa and their hallowed canyon.

But while their fellow Native Americans have honored the Tonowa claims to their ancestral heritage, the US Department of the Interior has not. Some years ago, during the early years of the Second World War, the federal government granted mining rights in the

Vega Towachi to Mammoth Steel, one of Western America's largest steel producers. Supposedly rich in iron ore, the tiny region was considered critical to the country's war supply efforts. Mammoth Steel crews moved onto the Vega's northern boundaries—and eventually into the sacred Canyon de Dios—displacing the Tonowa from their homeland. It is said that the tribe had scarcely vacated the valley, before the miners began their heartless work of destruction, obliterating half the mountain, including the mouth of a cave—the most hallowed shrine of the natives.

It was then that a curious incident occurred on Oscura Mesa that has never been fully explained—and that purportedly resulted in the deaths of dozens of men. Unconfirmed whispers of testimony, including miners and Indians alike, tell a myriad stories—from the attack of a prehistoric monster to the invasion of alien creatures to a failed government test project to the uncovering of a secret Nazi plot. None of these stories have ever been substantiated; all official records have been carefully laundered, and inhabitants of the area, to this day, are very reluctant to discuss the issue. At all levels, the truth of the incident seems to be veiled in a cloak of silence.

What is known for certain is that in 1943 a suit was filed in the ninth Judicial Court of Appeals in San Francisco, California. The case—The Tonowa Tribe vs. The United States of America—was represented by Lilia Bluelake on behalf of her people and was quickly and quietly settled out of court between the claimants and the defendant. The particulars of the case were sealed by the court and the federal government.

"The files have since disappeared," said John Harper, an investigator into the events. "The entire incident must have been very embarrassing to both the US government and to Mammoth Steel to induce them to such lengths of secrecy. We may never know what happened up there."

There are those who do know. Among them are Bluelake, (now Lilia Bluelake Hayden) who continues to serve as attorney for the Tonowa, and her husband, renowned animal collector, Matt 'Hunt 'em and Hold 'em' Hayden. Mr. and Mrs. Hayden own a small ranch south of the Canyon de Dios, and both were on the reservation when the 1943 events occurred. The famed hunter's presence, in particular, gives some weight to the rumors of efforts to subdue a huge beast, which is said to have roamed the Oscura Mesa.

"Was there some kind of creature you were hunting in those canyons?" he was once asked directly.

In answer, Hayden merely laughed as he shook his head. "If there were a monster on the Vega Towachi," he assured the interviewer, "I would have caught him."

As for Bluelake when she was asked if she could share anything about the mysterious events or the shadowed case, she paused and breathed deeply of the desert air with a sparkle in her eye. "Those days are past us now," she said. "A lot of things are—a lot of things that aren't important. It's time to go forward. The future is what matters."

However, a few details of the settlement worked out by Bluelake and the court have surfaced. And they have come to matter plenty. On the day following the settlement, Mammoth Steel ceased mining operations and was ordered by the Department of the Interior to evacuate the disputed area without compensation. No appeal to the decision was ever filed and within a year the company filed for bankruptcy. By a separate, but no doubt related mandate, the federal government restored the Tonowa to their ancestral homeland and awarded the tribe with irrevocable title to the Oscura Mesa.

Stories, taking the flavor of legend, have persisted regarding the Vega Towachi and more particularly the Oscura Mesa, where to this day the Tonowa continue to dwell and where they have painstakingly cleared mining debris and rubble from the buried cave in the canyon wall. The center of their peculiar worship, the cave is today a sanctuary to the god the Tonowa have worshipped for a thousand years.

And that god seems to have favored them. In the fifteen years since the Tonowa returned to their homes, that people have turned the forbidding "Canyon de Dios" into a lush desert oasis, and one of the largest and most productive cooperative farms in the Southwest. It is an anomaly on the desolate Navajo Reservation and a marvel to agriculturists who have come to wonder with awe at how the Tonowa have made the desert "blossom as a rose."

"It is not too difficult to understand," explains Thomas Running Wolf, the "Hawate" (or hereditary holy man) of the Tonowa. "If you believe in God, you believe in miracles. And our god has been good to us." When asked about the prehistoric creature of local rumor (a vengeful, armor-skinned bear known in Indian folklore as the Nyah-Gwaheh), Running Wolf just smiled. "We believe in God," he clarified. "We don't believe in monsters."

However, the Naya-Gwaheh is the most irresistible and enduring of the legends that continue to circulate in the lore of the Vega Towachi. It is also the most popular explanation of the violent events that are said to have occurred there in 1943.

Of those events, one interesting scrap of evidence does exist to confirm the legend of the armor-skinned monster. Surviving in the collection of photojournalist Charles "Buck" Buchannan is the fuzzy image of a ferocious, naked, bear-like face against the backdrop of rock. Recently displayed in Buchannan's Chicago exhibit, "Images of the Wild," the award-winning photograph is a singular portrait of horror. However, Buchannan himself has been consistent in his commentary of the picture. "I have never claimed that that image was anything but a double exposure of a grizzly bear and a cave wall—a delightful accident that created a particularly horrifying result. I wish it were a monster. That's one photo of wildlife I don't have."

Nevertheless, the legend has taken a life of its own as it has lapsed into folklore. Mike Thatcher, a long-time resident of the area and a neighbor to the Tonowa, had his own take on the monster of Oscura Mesa. "Maybe all the stories are a little bit true," he mused. "This is the southwest desert where all kinds of mystical and mysterious things happen. That is the beauty and romance of this land and these people. And both of 'em have a destiny."

Another former resident of the area who once lived at the Thatcher Ranch and continues to visit the Vega is Joseph Schindler, respected paleontologist, Associate Director of the Smithsonian Institution, and Curator of the institution's Natural History Museum. In fact, it was here on the reservation that Schindler formed and developed his theories of development of species on the Western Hemisphere—theories that finally took hold in scientific circles after the war.

When asked about such a species as the Nyah-Gwaheh or Great Armored Bear, Schindler responded with typical academic objectivity. "If the existence of such a creature could be proved, it would affirm many of the theories that we believe concerning the primordial development of life on the American continents. And that absolute proof may yet be discovered by a younger generation of explorers with courageous hearts and open minds. In the meantime, we adhere to theory based on the clues we have—and we continue to search. Science, after all, like religion, is a matter of faith. We all have to believe in something. And in a sense, we all worship something."

What the Tonowa have chosen to worship seems to be the key to the mystery of Oscura Mesa. And that key is locked in the hearts of these devout Native Americans and their connection to the infinite. The circumstances surrounding the enigmatic incidents of 1943 will probably never be known—not because they are secret, but because they are sacred. The Vega Towachi is a land rich in the intangible elements of the soul, veiled in the sacred devotion of a humble people. Perhaps that is all we need to know. And such is an appropriate testimony to the Garden of the Gods.

DISCUSSION QUESTIONS

1. In the beginning of the book everyone seems to have a different motivation for going into the cave. In what ways do Matt, Lilia, Tom, and Schindler's motivations differ? In what ways do they overlap?

2. Science and religion go head to head throughout the story. At what point in the book does one become more important than the other? Does this shift happen at different times for different characters?

3. Discuss the correlation between culture and privilege as it relates to the Tonowa people, as well as Mammoth Steel.

4. Lilia feels disconnected from the Native American culture in which she was born, as well as the "white world" she tried to acclimate into; but in the end she appears to have found her place. Does she commit to one culture more than the other?

5. The Nyah-Gwaheh serves as more than an angry beast. In what ways is he symbolic of the Tonowa people and their cultural fight?

6. Originally, "Bring em' back Alive Hayden" is simply a hired gun to help Schindler prove the beast exists. At what point does his quest go from professional to personal?

7. Before entering the cave, the Hawate asks Matt if he is "pure in heart." What was meant by this, and how does it shape Matt's actions in the future?

8. What is the conflict in this story between man and faith? Between man and nature? Between man and man?

9. How does the author utilize the concepts of light and darkness in the first chapter and throughout the book?

10. How does the author bridge the gap between reality and fantasy?

11. What character do you identify with or like the most?

12. What statement does the story make about the simple, life-changing power of a personal relationship with the Infinite amidst the turmoil of life?

About the Author

Stephen J. Stirling was born in Los Angeles, California, and grew up in the Southeast LA semi-ghetto of Huntington Park. He earned a bachelor's begree in journalism in 1976 and then spent the next few years wandering America in search of adventure. Interspersed through his college career and days on the road, he served a mission in Chile and taught for eight years as an early morning seminary teacher for the Church of Jesus Christ of Latter-day Saints.

Following graduation, Stirling settled in Chicago, where he entered the profession of advertising, a field in which he ultimately held many positions with companies from the Midwest to the Pacific Coast. He eventually planted roots in Orange County, California, where he establish Stirling Communications and spent fifteen years as a freelance copywriter, scriptwriter, and video producer.

In 1994, Stirling was hired by the Church Educational System and relocated with his family to Gilbert, Arizona, where he has fulfilled a lifelong dream of teaching released-time seminary for the past twenty-two years. He and his wife, Diane, were married in 1981 and are the parents of five children—Jennifer, Lindsey, Brooke, Marina, and Vladimir.

Stirling is the author of several books, including the humorous *Ultimate Catalogue*, and more recently, *Shedding Light on the Dark Side*, an in-depth exposé from the prophets on the nature and reality of Satan. Two years ago he published his first novel, Persona Non Grata, the first in a five-part series. Garden of the Gods is his second enthusiastic entry into the world of general market fiction.

Scan to visit

http://www.stephenjstirling.com/

0 26575 19387 9